WORTH THE *Weight*

A LOVE LIKE NO OTHER

KEISHA WRITENOW ALLEN

MIAMI, FLORIDA

WORTH THE WEIGHT: A LOVE LIKE NO OTHER

This book is a work of fiction. Names, characters, and incidents either are the products of the author's imagination or are used fictitiously, and any resemblance to actual persons, living or dead, events, or locales is entirely coincidental.

WORTH THE WEIGHT:
A LOVE LIKE NO OTHER

Copyright © 2021 by Keisha WriteNow Allen
All rights reserved. No part of this publication may be recorded, stored in a retrieval system, or transmitted in any form or by any means, electronic, mechanical, photocopying, recording, or otherwise, without the prior written permission from the publisher.

Paperback ISBN: 978-1-7355789-0-3
ebook ISBN: 978-1-7355789-1-0

Published by Kreative Kreations Publishing, LLC
Miami, FL

Printed in the United States of America
First edition: September 2021

Cover and Interior Design by: Carlyle Webb
Editing by: Brenna Davies
Interior Layout by: Jose Pepito

CONTENTS

Prologue: Broken Songbird Wings ix

Chapter 1	Meet My Achilles Heel	1
Chapter 2	My Friends are Better than Yours	10
Chapter 3	Iya Knows Best	17
Chapter 4	Sisterly Love	 24
Chapter 5	Liar Liar	 29
Chapter 6	Leon, is that You?	 34
Chapter 7	Dumb Bitch	 43
Chapter 8	Cry Long, You Cry Wrong	 48
Chapter 9	Gettin' my Groove Back	52
Chapter 10	Is that a Tickle in my Throat?	 57
Chapter 11	I'll Sleep When I'm Dead	 63
Chapter 12	Check Yo'self Before You Wreck Yo'self	 71
Chapter 13	It Ain't No Fun if My Homies Can't Get None	 77
Chapter 14	Don't Wake Me Because I Must be Dreamin'	 86
Chapter 15	Sharing is Caring	91
Chapter 16	Thanks for Giving	 96
Chapter 17	The Devil is a Liar	101

Chapter 18	Oh, Hell Nah!	108
Chapter 19	How's Your Eye?	113
Chapter 20	Bring That Ole Thing Back	117
Chapter 21	I'm on my Own	123
Chapter 22	On Bended Knee	130
Chapter 23	The Intervention	138
Chapter 24	Where do Broken Hearts Go?	148
Chapter 25	Be Careful What You Ask For	155
Chapter 26	So Long, Farewell	162
Chapter 27	Ready for War	172
Chapter 28	Panic No More	177
Chapter 29	How You Like Me Now?	185

Epilogue: I is Married Now! 193
Acknowledgements 207
Questions and Topics for Discussion 209

To my parents, but a special thanks to my mother: the backbone, the overcomer, the giver. She has the biggest, most loving and giving spirit of anyone I know. Thanks for loving me the way you do.

To my ladies who stayed longer than they should have in bad situations … This is for us.

*"Words are powerful. Be careful about the ones
you choose to believe about yourself."*

PROLOGUE

Broken Songbird Wings

How did I get here? I asked myself as Monique and I sat across the street from Terrence's house. I was supposed to be the good girl, the straight-laced sister, the one who got straight A's, stayed a virgin until I was twenty-two, and got a career doing what I thought would give prestige and make me look good. I figured if I wasn't going to have the body, at least I could have the brains; but there I was, doing exactly what I promised myself I would never do. My name is Anisa, and this is my journey.

First grade, six years old: I sat in Mr. Glen's reading class staring at Leon. I'd had a crush on him from the first time he walked into Mr. Glen's class, and I had finally worked up the nerve to write my letter: *Hey Leon. I really like you. You are so cute. Do you like me too? Check the box yes if you do, or no if you don't.*

I slipped the letter to my friend Coco, and she slid it to him.

Shortly after, Leon looked up at me and scowled as he wrote something on the paper. He folded it and handed it back over to Coco, who passed it back to me. My heart pounded as my chubby fingers opened the folded paper. It had a big red check on the NO box. Underneath that, it read, *I don't went your fat as.*

Dumb bastard couldn't even spell.

I spent the rest of the first grade embarrassed about the first time I got rejected, and it didn't make it any better when every time I would walk by Leon and his friends, they would look at me scornfully and crack up laughing. I felt like I was the biggest joke of the entire school.

One year later, at my Auntie Jackie's house for Auntie Jackie's birthday party—as I sat in the living room playing with Nia, Talia, and our dolls—I heard my mom and my aunt talking.

Auntie Jackie: "Amina, the girls are getting so big."

Mom: "Yes they are, and they're just the sweetest little things. They're super smart, too, especially my Anisa. She brings home nothing but straight A's."

Auntie Jackie: "Yes, I hear you, but that Nia is just gorgeous. She's so slim, and she looks like she's going to be tall, too. You should consider putting her in modeling."

Mom: "All my girls are beautiful, Jackie."

Auntie Jackie: "Yes, of course, but Anisa and Talia will never be models."

Mom: "They can be anything they want to be. I would never discourage them if that's what they wanted to do."

Auntie Jackie: "That's all good and well, but you need to

prepare them for the real world. They're pretty girls, but you need to put Anisa and Talia on a diet."

Mom: "Excuse me? We eat healthy, thank you very much."

Auntie Jackie: "Well, why are they so fluffy? Maybe you should have them play outside more."

Mom: "Jackie, I'm going to need you to stop talking like that about my children."

Auntie Jackie: "I'm just saying."

Mom: "Jackie, I'm not playing."

Auntie Jackie: "Okay, okay!"

When I got home that night, I stared at myself in the mirror. *No one is ever going to want you, and you're never going to be a model. You're a fat ass.*

After that night at Auntie Jackie's house, I resolved to be the smartest fat girl around. I dove headfirst into my school work so that I could get into the college of my choice, and since I didn't feel skinny enough to go out, my room became my refuge where I would watch television for hours on end.

Music videos became my obsession, and I was amazed with Whitney Houston, Lauren Hill, and Brandy, and the unique way they could manipulate their voices. In the years that followed, I became more fascinated with music and spent time in my room teaching myself the intricacies of doing runs and training my voice.

I would stand in front of the bathroom mirror and press my hand on my stomach, making sure I was breathing correctly. Although I hated what I saw in the mirror, I realized that I had some pipes; so, when I didn't want to look at myself, I'd close my eyes and belt out a song.

By the time I was twelve, my mother also learned that I could blow. One day, I couldn't help myself while riding in the car with her and my sisters on the way to school, and when I heard Deborah Cox's "Nobody's Supposed to Be Here" on the radio, I started singing along with the track, and my mother damn-near swerved off the road when I hit the high note. She pulled over, and we all stared at her like she was out of her mind. She turned the radio off and said, "Sing that again."

I was confused and even slightly embarrassed, so I asked, "Sing what?"

"That same song that you were just singing." I blushed because all eyes were on me.

Now, please understand, all of the singing I had done previously was reserved for the shower and my room. In fact, Talia was probably the only one who had heard me sing before because we shared a room. Sometimes, she would be my fake audience member of one and cheer me on. She'd say, "My sister's going to be a star." Unfortunately, I couldn't see past what I saw in the mirror.

When I sat there, staring at my mother blankly, she said, "Better yet, follow me and do everything I do." She sang Deborah Cox's song, and I sang along with her. I was even able to hit a few of the notes better than she did. She sat in stunned silence until Nia reminded her that we were going to be late for school. She got back on the road and got us to school, but when I went to get out of the car, she grabbed my arm gently. "Anisa, hold on, queen."

She looked at me with tears in her eyes. "Baby, you have something special, and I'm going to bring it out of you." She smiled at me and kissed me on the cheek.

I never paid what she said any mind that day. After that, I got annoyed when she wanted me to stand in front of everyone at the house and sing; I didn't like everyone looking at me. She even offered to get me voice lessons because she figured that would help me become comfortable, but I was upset with her when she kept asking me to perform. Eventually, she backed down. I wish I would've listened to her back then, because it damn sure would've saved me a lot of anguish down the road.

CHAPTER 1
Meet My Achilles Heel

22 years later

I slammed the phone down on this man for the second time this week. This was the third time this cheating man had stood me up in the past seven days, so now I'd be spending another Friday night alone. This time, his excuse was that he forgot he had his son tonight. Yeah, right. My head didn't get this big from being stupid. Things had started out wonderfully with us, and I'd been dating Terrence for almost three years, but lately he'd been finding ways to curve me. Within the past several months, I realized he was spending less time with me, and I presumed more with the mother of his child.

I was twenty-nine, and my thirtieth birthday was

approaching in a little over a month. I was ready to get married and start a family and had given this man almost three of my best years, and I'd be damned if he jumped ship now. I didn't want to do a drive by on him, but I could feel my angst growing by the second. I'd made up all kinds of scenarios in my mind as to where he really was, and I knew if I saw him with his baby's mom, Asha, that night, I was going to have to hurt him.

Okay, so let me back up.

I met Terrence on a girls' movie night in with my besties, Jamie and Monique, and my sisters, Talia and Nia. I could actually thank Nia for meeting Terrence, because she forced me to go out that night. We decided to do a chick flick theme at my new house with *Love and Basketball*, *Love Jones*, and *The Notebook*. I had plenty of wine on tap, and we were excited to get our drink on, but as I went to open the bottle, Nia said, "Oh shoot, I forgot to bring the wine opener!" I had literally just moved into my own place, so things were still in boxes, and I had no idea where mine could be at that moment. Leave it to Nia's ass to forget to do what she was supposed to.

Nia is my big sis, but you couldn't tell from the way she behaved. She was thirty-two, and she wanted but couldn't have children. She was unhappily married and a flight attendant. She had an unfaithful husband whose behavior she continually excused. She would say, "He wants children, and I can't give him any. What do I expect?" Every time I heard her say that, I would cringe.

"There's a lot of ways to have children," I told her, but she wouldn't listen. Out of the three of us, she was considered the prettiest—at least, according to the attention she got from men every time the three of us went out together. She was tall and slim but extremely shapely and would constantly attract all kinds of men. I was actually surprised she chose to settle down when she did, and with whom she did, because she could've had any man she wanted. In high school, she dated several of the football players, while I rarely even got a second glance from most of the guys. Schoolwork wasn't her thing, but she was popular—not only because she was pretty, but also because she was a flagette in the band.

We were complete opposites. I had all honors classes, was a shy wallflower, and never dated, and even though I was encouraged to join school extracurricular activities, they never interested me. Nia had her own set of friends because I started high school when she was a senior, and at times she pretended not to know I existed when we passed each other in the hallway. I don't think I ever quite got over that because if my own sister wasn't going to look out for me, who else would?

"Damn, Nia," I fussed. I loved my sister to death, but she got on every last one of my nerves. She wasn't responsible and had spent most of her life getting by on her looks. I know it's messed up, but I'd always thought maybe that's why God didn't give her any children; honestly, I didn't see how she would care for them if she couldn't remember something so simple. While my family was pretty tight knit, she and I weren't close because we didn't see eye to eye on much, and I silently envied that she could eat what she wanted and still look the way she did while I had tried almost every diet on the planet and never lost more than a few pounds.

I made a quick announcement: "If anyone has a wine opener, can I please borrow it?" Of course, no one did, so I threw on a pair of sweats, a cap, and some sneakers, because I'd be damned if we weren't going to drink that night.

I had a tough week at work. I found out that Bonnie, the woman who made partner at the law firm, had only started a year prior and didn't know shit. I suspected she was sleeping with the CEO, but I digress. My good friend and work buddy, Devyn, agreed that there was definitely something up with the one-stop-shop law office that we worked at because they never did anything by the book. They just made up their own rules as they went along.

So, back to the night I met Terrence. I decided to go to the local Target—that way I could also pick up some wine stoppers. I ran in the store and refused to pick up a hand basket, but as usual, I ended up picking up more items than I had intended. I hated when I did that. I fumbled with my car keys, a pack of maxi pads, a bottle of Watermelon Tropicana juice, a wine opener, a wine stopper, some hair oil, a pack of candy, and a bath sponge to get to the register. Sure enough, I dropped my pads and my car keys slid across the floor while I was standing in line. When I bent down to pick everything up, there he was. His kind eyes greeted me.

"Excuse me, miss. Do you need some help?" he asked.

Hell yeah! I thought. This brother could help me at any time. He was a gorgeous something with deep dimples and a beautiful smile, and he was six foot one of fine. He bent down and picked up my keys and pads as I half drooled at all his gorgeousness.

He spoke again. "Are you okay?"

I realized I hadn't spoken back. *Say something, dummy!*

He chuckled and put my pads on the checkout counter and handed me my keys. "Well, have a good night, beautiful."

Was he talking to me?

I finally found my voice. "Umm, thank you so much."

He turned back around and studied me briefly. "Anytime."

I finally got my bearings and purchased my items, but as I walked out of the store, there he was again, standing by the door. It looked like he was waiting for someone. For me?

"Excuse me," he said.

I cleared my throat so I could at least try and speak this time. "Umm, yes?"

He got a little closer. "I couldn't help but notice you."

I began to sweat under all of my clothing. Was he making me melt? I couldn't tell, but nonetheless, I couldn't believe he was actually checking for me like that.

Okay, so let's get this straight. I was cute, but you know the cute in the face, thin in the waist part? That's where you lost me. I was five seven, two hundred and thirty pounds. There was nothing thin about me, and I completely despised the pitiful look with the "You have such a pretty face, but I see you more like a sister" comment that some men would give me.

I adjusted my sweatshirt because I felt like I was suffocating.

"Who, me?" I asked. I could've kicked myself.

He chuckled again and licked his lips. I'm glad he found me funny. "Yes, you."

Man, don't you lick your lips like that. "Umm. Okay."

He continued, "I would love to take you out. I mean, if you're available."

In that moment, I did cartwheels, back flips, and splits in my head. *Hell yeah, I'm available!* I squeaked out a simple, "Yes I will … I mean am. Available, that is."

"Well, great!" He continued, "I'm Terrence. And you are?"

I'm in trouble, that's what I am. "Oh, my name is Anisa."

"Anisa, huh? Beautiful name for a beautiful lady. May I have a phone number?"

Baby, you could have all my numbers. My social security number, my birth date, my credit score … "Umm sure," I answered. I stood there, staring at him like an idiot, while he pulled his phone out.

"So, what is it?" he asked.

Before I thought about what I was saying, I answered, "What is what?" Again, I wanted to kick myself.

This time he laughed hard. "Your phone number. Remember, I just asked you what it was?"

I felt myself flush. It's amazing how someone who had an IQ of 148 could be acting this dumb.

I caught myself and tried to clean it up. "I apologize. I've just had a really long day."

"No worries." He cheesed at me and handed me his phone so I could enter my number.

We said our goodbyes, and he assured me he would call me soon. *Yeah right,* I thought, but as soon as I got back to my car, my phone rang.

"Hello?" I answered hesitantly.

"Hey, Anisa," his baritone voice crooned. "I just wanted you to have my number and let you know that it was an absolute pleasure meeting you this evening. I hope to see you sooner than later."

I lit up like an overdone light show on Christmas. "I would like that," I managed.

When I got back to the house, the ladies were fixing plates of food to take with them when they left. "Damn, Anisa," Jamie mused. "We were getting worried. We thought you had gotten kidnapped."

I smirked and checked my phone ... No missed calls. They couldn't have missed me that much. I said, "Chile, this is the one time that I would tell you not to come look for me." I filled them in on my new potential boo over our wine that night, and we never quite got through the rest of *Love and Basketball*. Not only had we all seen it a million-and-one times, but they thought my story was more entertaining.

So, why did I want to hurt Terrence now? I found out after we began dating for several months (six months to be exact) that Terrence had messed around and gotten some chick pregnant. That hurt me to my core. I almost lost it to know that not only did he cheat, but I wanted a family with him and he was having one with someone else. When I threatened to leave, he begged me to stay and promised she meant nothing to him and there was nothing we couldn't overcome. He swore up and down she had tricked him into sleeping with her that one time without a condom and just like that, she became pregnant.

"Fool, it only takes one time!" I exclaimed.

"Yeah, but she said she was on birth control."

I couldn't believe that a thirty-year-old man in 2017 was still falling for that line.

I was desperate. "What about an abortion?" I suggested.

He shrugged. "Out of the question for her."

"I'm sure it is," I mumbled.

Now, Terrence might've been a low-down, dirty cheater, but he was a financial advisor who didn't play about getting his money. His investments in the stock market and real estate didn't hurt either. When I first brought up marriage, he assured me we would get married once he got everything in order. According to him, several months before the baby news, everything was on the up and up, and he would be a millionaire in a few years, so I couldn't understand why he hadn't asked me to marry him yet.

"Christ!" I shouted. "How could you be so careless! Ugh! I hate you!" I grabbed my things and stormed off as he followed me outside.

"Baby, please don't go! I love you!"

That caught me off guard because he rarely said those three words to me. I mean, men don't use those words unless they really meant it, right?

I pouted and folded my arms. I probably should've put on my investigator's hat, or maybe took this as a clue to run, but I simply said, "I need some time to think." I convinced myself I was never going back, but after a few days of being home alone, I realized that not only was I not getting any younger, but I really loved this man. I decided his punishment was that he wouldn't touch my body for the next few weeks. *Yeah, that'll teach him,* I reasoned, but I began to think it didn't matter because he was probably getting it from somewhere else.

CHAPTER 2

My Friends are Better Than Yours

The next afternoon, after Terrence stood me up again, I decided to Facetime Jamie so I could vent. Surprisingly, she answered. And, as usual, she was working out.

"Hey, girl. What it do?" she said, slightly out of breath.

"You seem busy. Am I disturbing you?" I asked.

"Just doing a quick run on my treadmill, girlie. You know I have to get it in whenever I can."

For what? You have nothing to lose but your mind. But hey, if I was as dedicated as she was, maybe I wouldn't have been unhappy about my appearance.

Jamie lived in New York, and we'd been besties for over

ten years. We were students at Howard University and had both been lost freshwomen (if you will) on campus. I was standing in the middle of the A building, trying to read the map of campus, when Jamie tapped me on my shoulder.

"Excuse me, do you know where Locke Hall is? I'm so damn lost."

I turned around and gawked at her. She had wild curly hair and was absolutely gorgeous. She was a few inches taller than me and very thin. She reminded me of an African queen. Her overall appearance instantly made me think that she could be a model.

I laughed. "Oh, that's funny. I'm trying to get there as well, but girl, I'm just as lost as you."

We both giggled. "Well, hell," she said. "Let's be lost together."

We both struggled to read the map of the campus and found Locke Hall together—after a few more wrong turns, that is. We were inseparable after that.

Jamie was laid back, born in DC, and was one of the sweetest people you'd want to know. As beautiful as she was, she wasn't one to rely on her looks. She was smart and I had gotten it right: she was definitely working on her modeling career and was of Ethiopian heritage. Her parents believed in education first, but she figured she could give equal effort to her brain and her body. Her efforts had paid off and now she was doing her thing in the modeling industry. She had recently began taking acting classes as well because she knew she was probably on the tail end of her modeling career. Surprisingly, though, as many men as she met, dating was not a priority for her. She wasn't sure if she wanted to get married or have children, so she spent a lot of time complaining about the multitudes of men vying for her attention.

"I just don't have time to devote to anyone," she'd complain. "Most men can't understand my lifestyle."

Go figure. That was one problem I would love to have, plus I knew that if the right man came along, she'd be singing a different tune, but I let her believe that if she wanted to.

She was neutral on my and Terrence's relationship, so I liked getting her point of view at times. Any time I would bring up something he did or didn't do, she'd say, "Only you know what you can and cannot deal with." I welcomed her unbiased opinions in times like these.

I remembered she had just done a photo shoot in Philly the day before.

"How was the shoot?" I asked.

"Girl, you know how these photo shoots are. They can be draining, and I drove back home last night, but I'm good. How are you?"

"Terrence stood me up again for the third time this week."

"What happened now?" she asked.

"Well, he *said* he didn't remember that he was supposed to have his son, but I think it was more than that."

"Like what?"

"I think he's cheating again," I answered.

"Well, damn, why do you say that?"

"I don't know, but he's becoming more and more scarce," I whined.

"Well, did you ask him what's going on?"

"No, I hung up on him when he cancelled our plans."

"Girl, you're going to drive yourself crazy trying to figure it out. Why don't you just ask him what's going on?"

I rolled my eyes. *She is too trusting.* "Because he's not going to tell me he's lying, Jamie."

"Hmm, well why are you with him if you don't trust him?"

Good point. "Because I love him and want us to work."

"Make it work then," she replied. As if it was that easy. *Ugh! She is not helping!*

"I can't make it work if he's not being faithful!"

"Well, find out if he's being faithful then."

Okay, so maybe I need another opinion.

"I hear you. Okay. Well, I'll let you do your thing and I'll call you later."

"Okay, hon, enjoy the rest of your day."

"And Jamie?"

"Yeah?"

"Don't tell Mo what we just talked about."

"Okay," she answered.

We disconnected the call and I felt even more lost than before I called her.

A few hours later, as I sat around flipping through my channels, I thought about what Jamie had suggested earlier. I mean, it sounded simple enough. *Maybe I should take her advice and give Terrence a call so we can talk about what's really going on.* I wrestled with my thoughts, but my stubbornness wouldn't let me pick up the phone. During my time of deep contemplation, my phone began to blow up with calls from my other bestie, Monique.

I let her calls go to voicemail, because while I loved Monique to death, I realized that her kind of advice was not what I needed at that moment.

Shortly after, I checked my voicemail.

"Girrrrl, I know you hear me calling you. Don't you make me come over there! What did Terrence's trifling ass do this time?"

I shook my head.

Dammit, Jamie. So much for not telling Mo.

Now, Monique was someone you didn't want to play with. She was the fighter of our group and when we were younger, she would compare herself to the character O-Dog from *Menace II Society*. "Young, Black, and didn't give a fuck." She was the complete opposite of Jamie and I met her in ninth grade, in Mrs. Diaz's Spanish class. She was a simple beauty, and five foot five of feistiness. She was thick but shapely with a huge ass that got her into trouble on many occasions when we went out. There were a few times when she damn-near fought a man when he touched her behind in the club.

She loved to scream, "You must've never heard of 'U.N.I.T.Y.' by the Queen. Man, you need to back the fuck up! You better respect me!"

I felt sorry for the poor bastard who didn't heed her warnings because she had no problem throwing blows if she had to. At first, she wasn't a fan of Jamie's because she didn't want to share me with anyone, but after a while she came around, and now the three of us are thicker than thieves. Monique was good people, but if you crossed her, you didn't know who you were going to get. Sometimes I was afraid to mention anything about Terrence to her because she disliked—no, she *hated*—his guts. There was no in-between with her. Either she liked you or she didn't, but when she loved you there was nothing that she wouldn't do for you. While she always enjoyed male company, she wasn't in a committed relationship because she wasn't sure if there was any man strong enough to handle her personality.

I decided to give Mo a quick update by Facetime. When she answered, she tilted her head sideways as she fussed, "Took you long enough!"

"Hey, Mo. How are you?" I smiled, ignoring her comment.

Thankfully, it worked, because she didn't continue to harp on me leaving her out of the loop. "Mm-hmm. Girl, I'm good. Just cleaning up around here. What's going on with you?"

I sighed.

"What's wrong, friend?" she prodded.

"Terrence stood me up again last night."

"Again? What was his excuse this time?"

"Just that he had forgotten he was supposed to keep his son."

Monique kissed her teeth. "Girl, isn't that like the third time this week? That's not something you forget. His ass is lying."

"That's what I said!"

She began to get riled up. "Well, what are you going to do about it?"

"I don't know. I told him I was tired of his foolishness and hung up on him."

"That's it? You need to check his ass!" she exclaimed.

"I don't know what to do anymore."

"What *we* need to be doing is a drive by."

"A drive by, Monique? Really?"

"Yeah, pull up on that fool! Post up and see what he's up to!"

If only she knew how many times I'd contemplated doing that today. "I'm not going to do that, Mo. What would I look like at almost thirty doing that crazy shit?"

"You'd look like a woman who's not taking a man's shit anymore. That's what you'd look like."

I shook my head. She was something else, but I knew what I was getting into when I called her. Yep, Mo stayed ready.

I sighed. "I just need to reevaluate our situation."

"No, you need to reevaluate why you didn't hurt him when he cheated on you the first time."

"True enough," I agreed. "Ugh! Why can't they just act right?"

"I don't know, but I can tell you what to do when they act wrong."

My doorbell rang. *Who the hell could that be?* I wasn't expecting anyone. "Mo, someone's at my door. You mind if I call you back?"

"No problem, girlie, you just let me know if and when you want to pay that fool a visit."

I chuckled. "Bye, Mo."

CHAPTER 3

Iya Knows Best

When I looked through my peephole, I saw my iya's smiling face. I cheesed because not only was she one of the few people I would ever allow to show up at my house unannounced, but it always amazed me that she knew what I needed without me even having to say a word. It was like we had some kind of cosmic energy. My mom loved it when we called her the Yoruba word for *mother*, and I knew she'd have plenty of advice, warranted and unwarranted.

I had the best of both worlds in her as she wasn't your typical mother. When we were growing up, she would walk about barefoot in her Bohemian garb. She was a statuesque beauty with flawless ebony skin and a toned body from all the yoga she did. She was a free spirit at heart who wore dreads and a ring in her nose, and she didn't eat meat because she wanted to save the animals.

Iya was also a jazz musician who could put some of the best singers to shame. She thought I'd be the one to follow in her footsteps because I could blow as well, but I didn't think singing was something I could do for a living. Unlike my iya, my nerves were bad, and when I got on stage, my heart would pound, my hands would shake, and I felt nauseous. The biggest problem was that I felt self-conscious about my appearance because of my weight.

By the time I turned eighteen, she would take me to the clubs and pull me up on stage with her. I could follow all of her riffs and the audience would *oooh* and *ahhh* as I belted out a Nina Simone or Billie Holiday tune. Sometimes she'd let me put my own flavor on it and sing some Jill Scott or Erykah Badu. The crowd would go wild. It's no wonder that when I chose to be an attorney over a musician, she was quite disappointed.

"Is that your passion?" she had asked.

"I wouldn't say it's a passion, but it's pretty cool. Furthermore, I'm not you!" I declared. "You were made for this. Not only do you sing well, but look at you! You're absolutely beautiful."

Her facial expression showed how hurt she was over my statement. "My daughter, you are one of the most beautiful, intelligent young women I know."

"You're supposed to say that, Iya," I cried. "You're my mom." I held my arms out to my sides. "Look how fat I am!"

She rushed over and hugged me. "Oh, my child. You're beautiful just the way you are. Beauty is not something you can only see from the outside. You have to feel it from the inside, and then it will radiate throughout. You just have to realize it for yourself, and one day you will."

We didn't talk about it much after that, but what she told me that night always stayed on my mind. I didn't quite get it, though. What was this beauty she was talking about?

I always admired how unafraid she was to live her life on her own terms. It was a wonder she ever got married and had us, since she was so free-spirited. She was actually the one who cheated on my father and was the reason for their divorce. She would drill it into our heads that true love was when a person accepted you as you are and didn't try to change you for his or her benefit.

Iya rarely let anything bother her, and the few heated conversations I overheard between her and my father usually started when my father insisted she get a regular job. On several occasions, my sisters and I pressed our ears against their room door with our mouths wide open as we strained to hear their words.

"That's not fair, Khalil. You met me in the clubs, and I let you know from the beginning that marriage was not something I wanted," I heard Iya say time and time again. "Let's be honest, the only reason we got married is because I got pregnant with Nia and you insisted we be married so we could be a *real* family and our children could have the same last name as both of their parents."

When they separated, she let us know the real reason for

their separation. Her truth was that she fought the marriage idea for a while but eventually convinced herself to give it a try. She wanted to leave him on several occasions, but with each pregnancy, it got harder, until one day she couldn't take it anymore. After thirteen years of marriage, she ended up sleeping with one of her band mates, Adebayo. Everything went downhill after that, and well, the rest is history.

She concluded that just because you love someone, it doesn't mean you were meant to be together. Needless to say, my father is not a fan of her and Adebayo's relationship, but she and Adebayo are still happily together. In an open relationship, of course.

When all was said and done, she concluded that human beings should not be confined to being with one partner for life. In fact, she called it inhumane. She claimed we should be free to explore free love. She was surprised that all three of her daughters wanted to be married, especially me, being that I was a divorce attorney, so when I told her how I was hoping Terrence would propose by my thirtieth birthday, she wasn't very supportive.

"You're still so young," she said.

"Mom, I'm no spring chicken. I'll be thirty in a few years."

"Yes, but why would you want to tie yourself down? Marriage is tough, sweetheart. You have the world at your fingertips. You can travel, meet different people. The world is your oyster."

"My oyster is getting stale, though," I stated. "I've been

single for way too long and it's time that I settle down and have some babies."

She sighed but left it alone because she knew that once I was determined to do something, there was no changing my mind.

When I opened the door, she smiled at me and greeted me with a tight hug. Jazz music was playing softly from her phone.

"Hello, Mommy," I sang.

"Hello, queen," she sang back.

"How are you? What are you up to today?" I asked.

"Oh, you know me. I actually saged the house, and I've been practicing for tonight's show at D'vine Restaurant and Lounge, so I hope you ladies can make it."

I had missed her last few shows fooled up with Terrence's tired ass, so I definitely planned to be there. "I wouldn't miss it for the world," I assured her as I walked over to my kitchen with her on my heels.

"Great, because I told all my friends you would be there tonight. How's my queen's day going?"

I sighed. "I could be better. I got stood up again."

She didn't answer at first, but I already knew she was not a big fan of Terrence. "Is that so? I guess I shouldn't be surprised. I really think you should be dating more than one man," she threw in. "I don't think his chakras are aligned with yours."

I rolled my eyes. "Would you like something to drink?" I asked as I opened my refrigerator and looked inside. "His chakras, Iya? Really? What do they have to do with him standing me up?"

"I'm fine, thank you, queen," she said as she leaned on my countertop. "All I'm trying to say is that I don't think he's a good fit for you. I told you to date more than one man, if only to find out what you really like."

"Mom, I'm almost thirty. I know what I like."

She paused. "Can I ask you something without you getting offended?"

"You always do," I answered as I held my glass up to my lips.

She continued, "How can you know what you like if you don't truly know yourself?"

I choked slightly on my drink and coughed a few times. *Ouch.* I thought about it for a moment as I recovered and lightly beat on my chest. "I have a good career, my own home, and friends and family who love me. I think I'm doing just fine."

"Yes, but do you love *you*?"

What kind of question is that? I pondered her question for a moment. I finally answered, "Of course, I love me."

"Okay, well I'm glad to hear that. Can I ask you just one more question?"

"Sure."

"Why do you put up with so much from a person who isn't taking care of your heart?"

There wasn't much I could say after that because I knew

exactly what Iya was talking about. I'd spoken to her often about Terrence's cheating and how he had basically been going ghost on me. She tried to stay neutral, but she couldn't stand when I cried over the things he had or hadn't done. At this stage of my life, she understood that I wanted only one man, and she was okay with that as long as she knew it was a man who would do what it took to add to my happiness, not take away from it.

I decided it was time for her to go and ushered her to the door. "Well, Iya. I have to get some things done around the house, but I'm excited to see you perform later."

"Okay," she said, smiling. "I'm excited too, queen. I've got some new stuff, so I'm excited for you to hear it," she said as she made her way out the door. "I love you! Bye for now."

"I love you, too," I answered before I closed the door. I knew she was probably praying that the universe removed Terrence from my life.

CHAPTER 4

Sisterly Love

The next afternoon, I met my loving but opinionated sister, Talia, for brunch at one of our favorite soul food restaurants. We always made it our duty to meet up like this at least once a month because both of us had extremely busy lives. At twenty-seven, she was the baby, but I swear she was the most mature of my sisters. My niece, Aaliyah, was crying when I walked up. Talia looked exhausted.

"Hey, Lia!" I said excitedly as I went over to hug her.

"Hey, sis! Hold on." She shot Aaliyah a look. "Aaliyah, I said give it to me!"

"No!" Aaliyah fussed as she attempted to hold on to her doll for dear life.

I laughed at the two of them. Aaliyah was getting big, and now that she could talk back, she was giving her mother a run for her money. "Hey, Aaliyah, how are you?" I asked, but she didn't look up as she continued to play with her doll. The chicken and rice in her plate was also scattered on the table and the high chair.

"I'm going to take her toy away because she won't eat her food," Talia said, looking at her sternly.

Talia was a happily married nurse with a beautiful two-year-old daughter and a baby on the way. She and I took after my father's side of the family. We were tight as glue and resembled each other so much that people would often mistake us for twins—not to mention we were both on the thicker side and heavy chested.

Talia retreated and waved Aaliyah off.

I laughed, "Aaliyah's keeping you busy, huh?"

"Girl! This is nonstop. She doesn't listen!" She reached down and put her hand on her belly. "I don't know how I'm going to deal with two at the same time."

I looked over at Aaliyah and nodded. "Well, you have about four and a half months to figure it out," I teased.

"Now that you have that big house, don't think I won't be dropping her off by you. It'll be good practice." She was joking, but not really.

"Girl, you know you two are welcome at any time." I hoped she wasn't serious because I wasn't ready to babysit a two-year-old by myself. I'd never tell her that, though.

"So, what's going on with you?" she asked.

"Oh nothing," I lied.

"Girl, bye!" She laughed. "I can tell you're upset about something. Spill it."

I wasn't sure if I was obvious, or if Iya had spoken to her.

I sighed and began, "I think Terrence is cheating again."

"Umph," she replied sarcastically. "I don't think he ever stopped."

Talia couldn't stand him, so much so that I made sure to rarely have them in the same room. She didn't have a filter and had no problem telling him how much of a low-down, dirty cheater she thought he was.

"Why do you say that?" I asked.

"My sis, I love you, but you're too smart to be this blind. This man cheated and had a baby on you and now he barely has time for you. What else do you think he's up to?"

I didn't want to believe it, but I figured she was probably right. I tried to justify my actions. "Girl, it's hard out here. I don't want to end up alone."

"You won't. It just might not be your time," she said.

I was so tired of hearing that, especially from married women. They had someone to love on them and hold them at night. I wanted the same.

"That's easy for you to say. You already have someone who loves you."

"Yeah, but I spent plenty of time alone, learning myself. If Darius wasn't right, I wouldn't have married him."

"I'm going to be thirty soon, Lia," I whined.

"And? Your point? Is that supposed to be old or something?"

"I want babies," I argued, but she wasn't trying to hear it.

"And you'll have them when the time is right. Girl, if it comes down to it, you better hit the clinic and put some of those suckers on ice. What is it you always tell Nia?"

I thought about it. "I don't know. I tell her a lot of things."

The sound of glass breaking startled us, and Talia and I jumped to action as we realized that Aaliyah had knocked over the pitcher of water on our table. We quickly grabbed our napkins in a fruitless effort to capture the water as it spilled from the table onto the floor.

Thankfully, some of the waitstaff rushed over to help.

Talia fussed and used one of the napkins in an attempt to dry off some of the water that had gotten on her and Aaliyah.

After managing to clean up, we sat back down in an attempt to eat the food on our table. She returned to her conversation with me. "So, where was I?"

"You were asking what I always tell Nia."

"Oh, yeah. So, you're always telling her there are many ways to have a child, right? Not to mention you've been telling her she needs to leave her no-good husband. Why is that any different from you leaving this loser? In fact, you don't have anything stopping you."

I knew she was right. All Terrence and I really had together was time, well … and I think love. I also knew my sister wasn't going to feel sorry for me about this. She always stuck by the motto, "If you don't like it, change it." She'd been telling me I needed to throw his ass out with the trash for a while now, so I didn't know why I thought today would be any different.

I changed subjects as I wasn't in the mood for this conversation. "On a lighter note, will you be able to come out to D'Vine's tonight to hear Iya perform?"

"Oh, most definitely. I made sure Darius knew to be home on time tonight because he's on daughter duty. I love my child, but it's his turn to watch Aaliyah."

When the waiter brought our check, I took care of the bill and decided to get going before Talia went back in on my love life.

"I have a few errands to run before tonight, so I need to get going. Do you need help with anything?"

She shook her head and said, "I got it, sis."

"Okay, then." I reached over and hugged her and then kissed Aaliyah on her forehead as she barely looked in my direction. "Well, hopefully I'll see you there."

"Okay … love you," she said.

"I love you, too." And with that, I hurriedly made my way out of the restaurant without looking back.

CHAPTER 5

Liar Liar

I was still doing everything to keep from calling Terrence. If he wanted to see me, let him make the first move. This week was tough, and it was hard not being able to share my feelings with my man. Just like that—*rinnng!* It was like he'd read my mind. Maybe my iya was wrong about our chakras not being aligned after all.

I decided to let the phone ring a few times before I answered. Four times to be exact. I answered like I was all out of breath from working hard. Shit, the most exercise I got today was from opening and closing the refrigerator door.

"Hey," I breathed. I hoped that my horrible acting was convincing.

"Well hello, beautiful," he answered like I hadn't just

hung up the phone on his ass the night before. I could never quite understand how the male species could pretend nothing was wrong like that.

"I thought you weren't going to pick up. You okay? You sound tired," he said.

Well, you could've been seeing me if your ass was available. "Yeah, I just got in," I lied. "Whew! Been running errands all day."

"Oh yeah? What kind of errands?"

Dammit, I hadn't thought that far ahead. "Umm, just stuff."

"Okay," he replied. "Well, I hope you were able to get everything done."

"Umm for the most part. I'll finish tomorrow."

"Okay, well hopefully I'll be able to get some time with you tonight. I haven't seen my woman in a whole week. I made arrangements for us to grab dinner at Mai-Kai's tonight and watch the show after. I'd love to make up for skipping out on our plans the other night."

Dammit, he always knew how to get me. He knew I was itching to try the food out and see a Polynesian show. "What time?" I asked.

"Dinner at 7:45, show at 9:00."

"Shit, tonight is Iya's show at D'Vine's at 8:00. Why don't we reschedule for another night?"

"I've been waiting for almost two months to get these reservations. I don't know when we'll get them again. Doesn't your mom sing there monthly? Just go the next time," he offered.

I hated to stand my mother up because, as I said, I'd missed seeing her perform for a few months now; plus, this was one of the few times that I got to hang out with her and my sisters at the same time, especially with Nia constantly traveling as a flight attendant and Talia now having to look for babysitters. It didn't take me long to conclude that they would understand, because love didn't come knocking on my door every day.

I said, "Okay, see you in a few hours."

I called Nia and Talia on a three-way call and held my nose as I told them I would have to back out of Mom's show tonight because I wasn't feeling too hot. Talia offered to come by and drop off some medicine, but I assured her I would be fine and that I just needed some rest. Nia was, well … just Nia. She didn't care one way or the other.

Next, I called Iya. She sounded sad but said she understood, and she told me she hoped to see me at her next show. "Feel better, queen," she said. I felt bad for lying to them, but a girl needed some affection, and I'd be damned if I wasn't getting some tonight!

I spent the next hour riffling through my closet to find the cutest thing I could find at the last minute. I wanted Terrence's mouth to drop when he saw me. I decided on a pair of jeans and a long-sleeve button-down top. Thank goodness it was chilly because at least I could cover my arms.

I showered and sprayed my body down. I put a little extra down there just in case I decided to give him some. I also decided to put my natural hair in a frohawk.

He rang my doorbell at 7:00 on the dot. I opened the

door with my makeup done to a tee to hopefully distract from my midsection hanging slightly over my pants.

Whew! That man, that man! I stared at him standing there with his jeans and blazer on. He reminded me of a cover of GQ. Oh yeah, mad at him or not, he was definitely getting the business tonight.

He grinned. "Wow! You look amazing."

I stepped aside for him to come in. He stepped past me and kissed my cheek. "Wow, and you smell amazing as well."

I blushed. "Thank you. Give me one second while I grab my purse."

When we got to his Audi, he opened my door and I glided onto the seat. Well maybe not glided; I was far from graceful, but I made sure to put my ass down first and then swing my legs around. I learned that from all those bourgeoisie videos Jamie had me watch. "Men like polished women," she would say.

As I looked over my shoulder to watch his sexy ass circle the car to get to the driver's side, I spotted something on the back seat out the corner of my eye. Was that a car seat? I mean, I knew he was a father, but I had never seen that thing in his car before. That opened up some wounds and I got all up in my feelings.

I didn't wait for him to fully get in the car before I went in on him. "So, when did you get that thing?"

He looked puzzled. "What *thing* are you talking about?"

I used my thumb to point behind me. "That."

He looked on the backseat. "What, the car seat?"

"Well, that's the only thing back there," I snapped.

He chuckled. "Okay. Well since I'm keeping Mikel more now, I have to have one."

I folded my arms and huffed.

"Look, I know this has been a tough transition for you, but it's tough for all of us."

"Mm-hmm." I pouted. You seem to be enjoying it quite a bit."

He sighed. "And what would you have me do? He's here now. I thought you were okay with this."

I angled my body so he could see my face.

"I will never be okay with this!" I snapped. I was surprised that seeing a car seat could stir up that amount of emotion. PMSing wasn't helping either.

He ran his hands down his face. "Look," he said. "Can we just enjoy ourselves tonight and talk about this later?"

No, I want to bitch now, I thought, but I decided to calm myself down before he changed his mind and I ended up dickless and hungry that night.

I took a few deep breaths and calmed myself. "You're right. This isn't the time."

He started the car and we headed out.

CHAPTER 6

Leon, is that You?

When we got to the restaurant, the place was crowded, so we chose to do valet.

I said, "Damn, you were right about this place being popular, huh?"

"Yep, I'm so glad you could make it," he replied. He grabbed my hand. "Shall we?"

I cheesed and proudly grabbed his hand as we walked in. Maybe it was just my imagination, but I felt the eyes staring at us as we walked through the restaurant. I always felt that way when I walked beside him. I didn't know if it was my own subconscious or me just feeling insufficient, but I didn't know how I managed to get this specimen of a man. Everywhere we went, women would stop and stare at him.

I even caught a few pointing at times. They would lean over and whisper to their friends, "Look at him. How did she get him? Why are they together?" Okay, so maybe I was embellishing. I never heard that, but I definitely felt it.

We were seated right in the front, close to the stage. I didn't know how he got those seats, but I was beyond ecstatic. What I didn't realize was how hot it would be when the dancers were performing and throwing and spinning fire. I was burning up! I tried to play if off, but chile, a sistah was sweating!

"You okay?" Terrence asked as I wiped a bead of sweat from my forehead.

Hell no, I'm about to faint! "Mm-hmm," I lied. *Maybe wearing these long sleeves wasn't such a good idea after all.* I rolled my eyes. Big girl problems.

The show was over by 9:30, and I was beyond ready to go by then, but I was glad this was something I could check off my list. When we got back to my house, he followed me to my door but didn't follow me inside. It was almost as if he was waiting for an invitation.

I looked back at him. "What's wrong?" I asked.

"I'm not going to assume you want me to stay the night." He paused. "I know that things have been … tough."

My body was yearning for him, and although the warning bells were going off in my head, my vagina had other plans.

I smiled. "Of course, I want you to come in. Why wouldn't I?"

He came inside and locked the door behind him.

"Give me a minute," I said.

I ran to the bathroom and did a quick wipe up because no one wants a sweaty cooch. I undressed and left my bra and underwear on and came back out in a long, thin robe.

When I came out, Terrence was sitting on the couch looking like a snack. I put my hand on my hip and did a pose for him.

He stood up and rubbed his hands together as he walked over to me.

"Damn, baby, I've missed you," he muttered as he found the opening in my robe and rubbed his hands up and down my legs and ass.

"I've missed you, too," I purred.

He gently kissed me. His lips were oh so soft. His kiss lit an inferno in me, and I felt myself melting. I grabbed his hand and pulled him toward my bedroom. We kissed some more. He was being a little too gentle because I was past ready. I didn't feel like being passionate; I needed to get fucked!

I put my hands in his soft hair, roughly brought his face back to mine, and basically shoved my tongue down his throat.

He pulled back and chuckled. "Damn, girl."

"Sorry, baby, but you shouldn't have kept me waiting for so long." I pushed him and he fell back on the bed.

He laughed. "Slow down, baby, I'm not going anywhere."

Shit, I'd heard that before. I walked over and stood before him as he sat up and opened my robe.

He whispered, "Damn, girl. All these dangerous curves on you."

I didn't feel curvaceous. How I really felt was bloated. I backed up a little. "Hold on."

I went to the light switch and cut all the lights off.

"Damn, baby, can I see you this time?" he protested.

I ignored him. He knew I wasn't comfortable with my body. I let my robe fall to the floor and put my breasts in his face.

He inhaled my scent and said, "You smell yummy."

I bent down so he could reach my bra, and he unclipped it and threw it somewhere. I pulled his shirt over his head and pushed him onto the bed then I leaned down and kissed him on his neck and chest. He moaned. I unbuckled his pants and helped him pull his pants down and take his boxers off. His erection saluted me.

He gently pushed me down onto the bed and got on top of me. He put his mouth on my breasts and neck and then ran kisses down my stomach but came back up. He slid my panties off, worked his finger on my clit and slipped two inside. I pushed his head down, because as much disappearing as he had been doing lately, he owed me.

He didn't budge.

Our sex life was good for the most part, but I was yearning for him to perform oral sex on me. Unfortunately, he'd never gone down on me during the whole time we dated. If I even hinted at him going there, he'd say, "God don't eat meat." What in the hell?

He massaged my clit until I soaked his fingers and moaned.

He knew I was ready. He got off me briefly and reached for a condom in his pants pocket. Now, that was the other thing I didn't understand. While I appreciated his wanting to be safe, we had been dating for almost three years, and he never wanted to have sex without one when it came to me. Yet, he obviously did it with his baby mama. I know he claimed it was only one time, but I was beginning to think that was probably a lie.

He kissed me again and entered me slowly. I opened my legs wider and wrapped my legs around him so he could get full penetration. He pumped and I matched every thrust as I held on to him for dear life. I wished it could always be like this. He was putting in work tonight. I don't think I'd ever seen him go this hard. I could see the beads of sweat beginning to form on his forehead as he worked the middle. It was almost like he thought this was the last time.

I screamed, "Oh yeah, baby. I'm cuming!"

He pumped harder and thrust faster.

"Yes! Yes! Deeper, baby, deeper!" I yelled.

He went deeper and I came hard. That was one of the best nuts I'd had in a while. He came shortly thereafter. "Damn, baby, that was good," he muttered as he rolled off of me, got up, and went to do his business in the bathroom.

His phone on the nightstand rang, and I looked over at it. A woman's picture appeared, but there was no name. It just said "A." I began to reach over to grab it when he flung the bathroom door open and damn-near broke his neck to get to it. He grabbed it up before I could say anything, then answered while stepping into his boxers and walked out of the room.

I could hear him speaking lowly in the hallway.

Oh, hell no, I thought. *Is he talking to another woman in my house? This disrespectful asshole!* Any fool could figure out what the A stood for. A for Asha, as in his baby's mom. I got up from the bed and threw on my robe. By the time I made it to the kitchen, he had the refrigerator door open and was looking for something in there and had the phone in the crook of his neck, smooth talking someone on the other end.

I fought the urge to grab one of the pots and hit him over the head like they did in the movies. "Who's that?" I asked loud enough so hopefully she could hear me as well.

He glanced up in mild shock. Apparently, he didn't think I would come out of the room. He said to the person on the line, "Hold one sec." He looked at his phone and tapped a button, and I figured that he muted the line. This fool had nerve. He ordered, "Hey, baby. Go back to the room. I'll be in there shortly."

Ugh ugh. Not tonight! "Who was that?" I asked again, this time more firmly, folding my arms.

He sighed, realizing that he wasn't getting out of this that easily.

"Just hold on," he muttered. "I told you I'll be right there."

I rushed into the kitchen and grabbed the phone, but he held on to it. We tussled with it until it fell and slid under the dining table. He was a second quicker than me and grabbed it up before I could get to it. He hit the *end call* button.

I was beyond pissed and stormed off toward the room as he followed close behind.

"Okay, look," he stated. "You want me to tell you the truth, I'll tell you the truth."

I spun around and shot him a look that let him know I wasn't playing.

"Let's go in the room and talk," he suggested.

"No, we can talk right here!" I snapped.

He closed his eyes, sighed, and then ran his hands down his face like he always did when we argued. "Okay. Sooo … that was Asha."

No shit, Sherlock. I wasn't surprised, I just wanted confirmation.

I held my breath because I wasn't sure I was ready for what he would say next. "Well, why are you trying to hide it if there's nothing going on between you two?"

He leaned against the wall and hung his head before he spoke. "Well, Asha and I've been talking …"

"Mm-hmm," I prodded with my hand on my hip.

"We … we … umm, were thinking about trying to make it work." He paused. "For Mikel's sake."

My legs went numb, and I leaned against the wall to steady myself. He reached over to help, but I put my hand up. I couldn't breathe. The room had suddenly gotten warm, and I kept my AC low.

It took me a moment to find my voice, but when I did, I

put my palm to my chest and whispered, "You never stopped messing with her, did you?"

He sighed and avoided eye contact.

"So, what was all this shit for tonight?" I asked.

"I wanted to tell you, I just didn't know how. I'm sorry, Anisa."

"Yes, you are … sorry, that is," I retorted. "When were you going to tell me. Before or after you fucked me?"

He didn't answer. He didn't need to. His silence was golden. There was nothing left to say.

Never had I felt so betrayed than in that moment. It was one thing to think he was cheating, but knowing he was leaving me for the woman he cheated on me with and had a child with was devastating. I never did anything more than love this man, and this is what I got?

I felt as if the air had been sucked out of the room as we stood in silence. The one thing I was proud of myself for was not letting him see a tear fall from my eye.

Finally, I yelled, "Get out, you lying, trifling muthafucka!"

He tried to interject, "Look, let's take some time and—"

"Now!" I shouted. I didn't want to hear anything else from him.

That must have hit a nerve, because his whole demeanor changed. He looked me up and down and smirked. "I was trying to work with you. I mean, look at you. No one is ever going to want you."

What? Flashbacks of the first grade came flooding back, reminding me of when Leon said he didn't want my fat ass. And here it was—Terrence was rejecting me as well. I couldn't believe he could utter those words to me. This man who claimed he loved me. This man who claimed he wanted to make it work. This man I spent almost three years of my life with.

In that moment, I was thankful for my dad's how-to-knock-a-fool-out-in-three-moves class that he taught me and my sisters for self-defense. Something came over me, and all I remember was seeing red. I balled my fist up, reached back with all my might, and tried to break his jaw. Apparently, he didn't see it coming because my first punch made him stagger, but I didn't stop there. He put his arms up to block my fury, but after a rapid succession of blows, he stumbled backward over my footstool and hit the ground.

I had missed his jaw but made a connection with his eye. He held his eye and cursed, "Damn, Anisa! Fucking bitch!"

I glowered at him as he shuffled backward and got up. He held his eye as he spoke.

"I need to get my keys."

I stood there numbly as he shuffled past me to the room. He came out a minute later, half dressed, and looked at me pitifully.

Before he walked out, he said, "I hope one day we can be friends," and shut the door behind him.

CHAPTER 7

Dumb Bitch

I couldn't sleep, and I cried so much that my lips and mouth were dry, and my eyes were red. I stared at myself in the mirror. I looked a mess. My mind replayed the night's events. I couldn't believe all of that had just gone down. Even though I was hurting, I knew I never should've put my hands on him, because I wouldn't want that done to me. I couldn't remember the last time I had even fought as Iya had always taught us to fight—with our words first. I was upset for letting myself get out of character like that.

Leon's words continued to play in my head. *I don't want your fat ass.* Then Terrence's words played in my mind. *No one is ever going to want you.* Maybe they were right. Who was going to want my fat ass? My greatest nightmare of being alone was coming true. I felt like an idiot for putting up with him for that long. Not only did I put up with his lies, but I had also lied to my family for him and missed Iya's show.

I was a dumb bitch.

I went to my bed and balled up in the fetal position while I held my pillow and cried some more. I didn't know how I was going to recover from this. Was I that unlovable? Why was the one thing I wanted so much seemingly running from me? Even though I hated him in that moment, I missed his body beside me. Damn, what was wrong with me? Was I glutton for punishment? I wanted to call someone. I thought of Monique so maybe I could take her up on that drive by, but I didn't have the energy. I decided to lie there and wallow in my pain.

Talia called. I let it go to voicemail, but she called again. I realized I'd better answer because she was probably calling to check how I was doing since I'd told her I wasn't feeling well the night before. God forbid she send the paramedics to my house.

I tried to make myself sound perky. "Hey, Lia!" I exclaimed.

"Hey, sis. I just wanted to check on you. I know you weren't feeling well yesterday."

"Oh. I'll be fine. I just need a few days."

"Yeah, you still don't sound too hot," she replied. "You sure you don't need me to come by and bring you something?"

"Oh no, no. I'll be fine," I assured her. "I just need some rest. Don't worry about me."

"Okay. Well, if you need anything, make sure to call me."

"Thanks, sis." I remembered Iya's show. "How was the show?" I asked.

"Oh my God!" she exclaimed. "It was soooo good! Iya had Adebayo playing the drums, and she had two new backup singers. She sounded amazing! I was so proud of her!"

Shit! Now I felt like an even bigger ass.

"That's great! I'm sorry I had to miss it."

"Yeah, I'm sorry, too, but she'll have more. You just make sure to be at the next one."

"I will," I promised.

"Well, let me get back to my family over here. I'm making Sunday dinner."

"Thanks again. I appreciate you," I told her and we hung up.

I hated my life.

I stayed in bed for the remainder of the day, getting up just to eat and pee. I brought a pack of tissues in my bed, watched Lifetime movies and reruns of *Insecure* on my DVR, ate, and cried. I found ice cream, cookies, chips, and anything fattening to munch on. Hell, I didn't care. No one wanted my ass anyway.

The next morning, I called out of work. I knew they'd be surprised since that was the first time in the three and a half years since I'd started working at the firm that I had ever called out sick. As a Black woman, I made it my business to work hard to get to where I was. Honestly, I knew I was a better attorney than most of those kiss-asses, but it felt as if I was going nowhere as far as advancement with this company. I was disgusted with my love life and my appearance, and now that I thought about it, I wasn't too happy with my career either.

I pulled the covers over my head and finally dozed off. I was awakened to the ringing of my phone. When I glanced up, it was 11:38 a.m. At least I'd managed to get a little rest. It was my iya. I decided to answer her call because I figured that was the least I could do after ghosting her last night.

"Hello, sunshine," she sang.

"Hey, Iya."

"Are you feeling any better?"

"The same," I lied. Well, technically it wasn't a lie. I wasn't physically sick, but I damn sure wasn't mentally well.

I changed the subject.

"Talia said your show was awesome, Iya. I'm so sorry to have missed it."

She said, "No, baby. No apologies necessary. You couldn't help being sick."

Damn. I could no longer hold in my tears. Lying to Iya was not something I could do anymore. "I'm so sorry."

"Oh my goodness! Sorry for what? Are you okay, queen?" she asked.

"No!" I cried. I was babbling, and I figured that I was almost inaudible at that point.

"Oh my God! What's wrong?"

I knew I was scaring her, so I decided to come clean.

"I'm a horrible person, and an even worse daughter," I cried.

"What are you talking about? Do you need me to come over?" she asked almost frantically.

"N-n-no," I stammered and blew my snotty nose. I came clean about how I had stood her up the night before for Terrence's bitch ass.

She didn't seem upset. She was more concerned for how I was doing than anything else.

"Okay, I'm coming now. See you in a minute." She hung up before I could answer.

She made it to my house in less than half an hour, but she didn't show up alone. When I opened the door, I was surprised to also see …

"Daddy!" I yelled. While I was happy to see him, I wasn't quite sure if I was ready to let him know what happened between me and Terrence because he didn't play about his girls.

Before even stepping inside, Iya wrapped her arms around me and held me tight as I cried.

CHAPTER 8

Cry Long, You Cry Wrong

One thing I could say about my parents was although they claimed to not like each other much, they always managed to come together when it came to their children. But when I said they were different, I wasn't kidding. I mean, they were total opposites.

My daddy was almost ten years older than my mother, and while she was the peacemaker, my father was something else. Like Monique, he had no problems putting paws on anyone that messed with someone he loved. My iya was flowers and butterflies, and he, well … he believed in bullets. He loved telling us how he'd spent plenty of time at the local gun range to keep his shooting skills sharp. "Just in case," he'd say. "Just in case." He'd almost caught a case a time or two in his younger days for shooting at one of his sister's boyfriends after he put his hands on her.

We enjoyed his many stories of how he was a proud up-and-coming Black Panther in the early '70s and used to go out to the rallies with his father as a teenager, so he believed in taking a hands-on approach with anyone that messed with his family.

He left the *soft shit* (as he called it) to my mother. When we would fall off of our bikes as kids, he would tell us, "Okay, that's enough crying now. Suck it up and get back on that bike." He didn't do well with excuses, even if you were sick and half dead. He was the one that would feel our heads when we had a temperature and say, "Your legs and brain still work, right? There's no reason for you to stay home today." Yeah, he was tough.

While my mother was consoling me, the first thing he asked was, "What the hell did that man do to my baby?"

He'd heard more than enough stories about how Terrence was treating me from Iya and Talia, so like with Talia, I couldn't bring him around Terrence because everyone knew it wouldn't have been good. He wasn't kidding either—my father never made empty promises.

I sniffled and rubbed my swollen eyes. "Daddy, I'm okay."

He said, "You don't look okay. What, have you been lying around here crying all day?"

He had hit the nail on the head. "Sort of," I answered pitifully.

"Well, it's time to get back up now. You know better than to let this punk keep you down."

I knew he was right, but that didn't keep the tears from falling again.

Iya interjected, "Khalil, give my child a break!"

He countered, "She's my child, too."

My mother gave him *the stare* and he backed down. He puffed out his chest and went to the kitchen. "You have something to drink?" he yelled.

"Yes," I squeaked. "I have plenty of juice in the fridge, and water and sodas in the pantry."

"No, child, I mean something real, like a Heineken or something."

My mother yelled, "Khalil, stop bothering this child."

He opened and closed my cabinets and then I heard him pop the top of one of the soda cans. He came back out while holding it to his head. After a few gulps he said, "So, tell us what happened."

I gave them the abbreviated version of what had gone down that night with Terrence. I made sure to include how I got him good in the eye when I punched him, though.

He nodded. "That's my baby. I'm glad that you handled your business. I see you put my how-to-knock-a-fool-out-in-three-moves class to use. You did me proud."

My mother rubbed her temples and glared at him. "What if he had hit her back? You know I don't promote violence."

His reply: "I wish he would've. That's the last thing he would've done."

Iya rolled her eyes and focused her attention back on me. She asked, "Do you need me to stay here with you tonight?"

"Amina, stop babying that woman," my father insisted. "She's grown."

I decided to intervene before they bit each other's heads off.

"I'm okay. Really … I just needed a moment to get it all out, but I'm fine. I really am."

Iya studied me. "You sure?"

"I'm positive," I answered and gave her a weak smile.

"Okay, queen, but if you need me, you just pick up the phone." She kissed my cheek and got up, and my father walked over and hugged me.

He spoke barely above a whisper, "Remember what I said. Don't let anybody steal your shine, beautiful, and good job with his eye." With a wink, he added, "I knew you had it in you."

"Khalil!" my mother yelled.

"Bye!" He kissed my forehead and followed her out the door.

When they left, I sat in silence for a few moments. Although my daddy was tough, he was right. Why was I sitting around worried about a man who treated me so horribly? It was time to do something different, and I wasn't going to waste any more time feeling sorry for myself. It was time to take a quick getaway, and I knew exactly where I wanted to go and who I wanted to go with.

CHAPTER 9

Gettin' my Groove Back

It was October, so most places in the United States would be chilly, and I figured it was too short notice to do an island getaway. It didn't take me long to realize it was Howard Homecoming weekend, though, and that was all the motivation I needed because DC was one of my favorite cities—not to mention, I hadn't been there in a while.

First, I called Jamie. She didn't have a nine-to-five like the rest of us, so I figured she'd be available. She answered right away. "Hey, hon."

"Hey, are you busy?"

"Not really. I just had to get these feet done. Whew, chile! I was a day over my two-week time frame."

I rolled my eyes. I guess it took a lot to stay beautiful.

Maybe it was a model thing. I was glad I didn't have those problems.

I asked, "You want to get away this weekend?"

"To where?"

"I'm thinking DC. I haven't been in years, and with all that's going on with Terrence, there's no better time than the present to go."

"Did something else happen?" she inquired.

"A whole lot, but I'll tell you about that later."

She paused. "Okay. DC is dope, and it is Howard's Homecoming weekend. Hmm. I might be able to make that happen. Let me check my calendar."

"Well, think about it and let me know by this evening. I'm going regardless, even if I have to go by myself."

"Wait, hold on," she said.

I heard a voice in the background utter something in another language, then she said, "Please keep your foot still. You mess up nail."

"Oh, my bad," Jamie apologized to whoever was doing her pedicure.

She laughed and came back on the phone whispering, "Girl, they cuss my ass out every time I come in here."

I laughed and shook my head. "Jamie, why don't you go to a Black-owned spa sometimes? We could use your business, too."

"I know, I know," she admitted. "But Linh's been doing my nails for years, and she hooks my shit up! Anyway, I'll let you know for sure about this weekend by this afternoon."

"Okay. Cool," I answered.

Next, I dialed Monique. I wasn't sure if she could get out of her government job on such late notice, but it was worth a try. Hell, she didn't want to be there anyway.

Surprisingly, she answered; it was rare that she picked up during work hours.

"Hey, Mo. I was going to leave you a message but I'm glad you picked up."

"Hey, bestie," she answered. "Yeah, my coworker is doing my hair."

I glanced at my watch. It was 3:13. "Oh, are you off today?"

"No, ma'am. She's hooking me up in the bathroom right quick."

I shook my head. "Wait, so you're telling me that you're getting your hair done at your actual job?"

"Yup."

I assumed maybe it was a quick updo. "What're you getting done to it?"

"She's putting in some big plaits."

"Mo, plaits take a while. How long have you been in the bathroom?"

"Mmm. About an hour now."

I slapped my palm to my forehead. *This woman is wild!* "Mo, don't you think they're going to notice you're not at your desk?"

"Girl, I've given these people five and a half years of my life. They'll be okay."

"Okay, Mo." I chuckled. Maybe she'd have the time to get away after all. Hell, she probably wouldn't have a job after today. "So anyway. I wanted to invite you to come with me to DC on Wednesday."

She paused. "It's Monday afternoon. How do you suppose I do that?"

I shook my head again. So, she could disappear for hours at a time when she was on company time, but had a problem calling out when she wouldn't be stealing time? "Mo, DC won't be the same without you. Can't you make something happen?"

The line went silent. I knew she was trying to figure something out because Monique never missed a good time.

"I'll tell you what," she offered. "I'll leave Thursday evening and call out Friday and Monday."

"That works, too," I agreed, "but I want you to know I plan to tour the National Museum of African American History and Culture in the day on Thursday."

"Damn, Nisa." I knew she was pouting. "You know I've been trying to get there forever now. Can't you go on Friday instead?"

I thought about it briefly. "I figure that Friday we'll be on The Yard, and you know that with it being Homecoming weekend, we're going to have a lot to do. It's going to be nonstop. I guess I'll see what I can do, though."

"Oh damn. Wait! The Yard!" Monique exclaimed. She'd been to Homecoming a time or two with me and Jamie, and she enjoyed all of the HBCU college experiences, so she definitely didn't want to miss any of the shows. She never went to college but always said she wished she had, if only to have the Black college experience.

She backed down. "Okay, never mind. I'll definitely be there. We can fly out together."

I laughed. "Are you sure? I thought you said you would come on Thursday evening and call out Friday and Monday?"

"Yeah, fuck that. I have plenty of sick time. Book my ticket to fly out with you."

"Okay, will do." I chuckled. I knew she'd see things my way.

CHAPTER 10

Is that a Tickle in my Throat?

I decided to take the rest of the week as well as Monday off from my job. I didn't care what they had to say because they didn't treat me right anyway. When I called my boss, Colin Abernathy, the next morning, he sounded genuinely concerned. He asked, "Have you been to the hospital?"

"No, sir."

"Well, I hope you're taking something for whatever you have. We miss you around here, so hurry up and get well so you can come back to us."

I'm sure they did. They loved to dump the cases no one wanted to deal with on me. I was basically the go-to for cases they knew were almost impossible to win. "Give it to Anisa," I heard kiss-ass Bill Turkey-Neck Cousins say one day. Everyone knew I had a better chance of becoming partner, so he was vying for my spot. Okay, so his name didn't really have *turkey-neck* in it, but his skin was super pale, and the skin on his neck was loose and red, kind of like a turkey. Devyn—one of the few other Black people at the company—nicknamed him that.

Devyn was one of the reasons I was still at this firm. Like me, he was a hard worker and was wondering why he didn't see much progress in regard to getting promoted at the firm, but he encouraged me not to give up because most of those idiots were just waiting for us to fail. He had a wife and a son and daughter that kept him from giving up. He'd say, "I'm fighting for my family and everything I stand for." I got it, but unlike him, I didn't have a family to take care of, so if I was going to make a move, this might be the best time to do it.

So back to Bill. He was one of the worst lawyers at the firm, and he somehow managed to always get the easiest cases. Even when I got a win when no one thought I could, he still found a way to hate on my work. "I would've gotten the client more money," he'd say. "You should've given the case to me." But everyone knew he didn't have the brainpower to get it done the way I did. In fact, the only thing he could do quicker and better was lie. I couldn't stand him. I'm sure he was in Colin's ear, telling him how lazy I was. Not being there for a week wasn't going to help my case, but in that moment, I didn't care. If he wanted my position, let him have it.

I told Colin, "Yes, I've done all of that. The doctor

suggested I take some time off and just rest." I coughed a few times to give it extra effect.

"Oh yeah, you do sound horrible," he said.

"Okay," I added. I coughed one more time. "I'm about to take this medicine and get some rest."

"Okay. Yeah, sure. You do that."

I hung up. *Yes!* I thought. That wasn't too bad. Maybe I had missed my calling as a thespian after all. I went through my drawers and closets to find my cutest outfits when the phone rang. It was Talia.

"Hey, sis," I answered.

"Don't *hey sis* me," she fussed. "How are you going to DC, and you haven't invited me?"

I laughed. "Sorry, sis, it was last minute. Not to mention, you have Aaliyah."

"Mm-hmm." She got quiet. I could tell she was waiting.

"And Terrence and I broke up, as you probably know by now."

She didn't try and pretend she was sorry. "It's about damn time!" she exclaimed. "What happened?"

It was still raw, and I didn't want to cry anymore, so I asked if we could talk about it another time. "In fact, ask Iya. She can tell you everything," I suggested.

"Okay. Well, I know it probably feels like the world is going to end, but he's not the be all, end all. You deserve much better."

"I know, sis," I agreed.

"Well, call me when you get back and have fun for me! Love you."

"Thanks, Lia. I love you too."

I packed my stuff and put everything by the front door. Tomorrow couldn't come fast enough. It was about to be lit!

Monique and I caught the 2:55 flight from Fort Lauderdale airport to Baltimore/National airport the next afternoon. My girl was a trip. She met me at my house with some tight-ass jeans on with thigh-high boots.

"Where you going?" I asked. "We're just getting on the plane."

"Girl, if you stay ready, you don't have to get ready," she said, laughing.

I shook my head and laughed along with her. This girl!

My excitement grew when the pilot announced we'd be on the ground in thirty minutes and I looked out the window and saw the ground below.

Jamie arrived at the Airbnb around 6:30 the next morning. She was excited about going to the museum because although she'd been before, it was so massive, she hadn't had a chance to finish. This was my third time since it opened in 2016, but I never got tired of learning about my culture. I also figured I would see something this time that I missed previously.

When we got to the National Museum of African American History and Culture, Monique's mouth dropped. We got on the elevator to take us down to the bottom, and she cheesed like a kid in the candy store as the museum docent gave us a brief rundown about how to get full gratification from what the museum had to offer.

I'm not saying this because I'm a Black woman, but this

museum was truly one of the best ones that I'd ever come across. There were eight floors in total, and the bottom floor was built to mimic a slave ship. Each magnificent level had a different theme that eventually brought you into present day. Each time I visited the museum, I experienced different emotions.

As we somberly made our way through the first few floors, I was reminded of the struggle that my people had been in since we were brought to this country. Seeing the South Carolina Slave Cabin and Emmett Till's pictures and casket evoked even more painful times in America's history and reminded me that although we'd come a long way, every day was still a fight.

As we went up each level, I was amazed to see things I'd missed on previous visits. Viewing Harriet Tubman's shawl made me feel strong, and seeing Black musicians that came before me and paved the way gave me a sense of pride. I stopped longer than necessary when I got to Oprah's couch. How did a poor Black woman from Mississippi (who looked like me) get the confidence and strength to do what she did? Where did that confidence and strength come from, and what was wrong with me? I had all this talent inside of me, but I wasn't doing anything with it. I was reminded that women can do whatever we put our minds to, and I hoped that one day I would find the courage to pursue and live out my greatest dreams as well.

After several hours of touring, we stopped to grab something to eat from one of the cafés in the museum. We toured a few more hours, but after eight hours, we were exhausted.

We took a Lyft back to our Airbnb and I filled the ladies in on what had gone down with Terrence. We spent the rest of the night reminiscing about old times because we knew that come tomorrow, we would be going nonstop.

CHAPTER 11

I'll Sleep When I'm Dead

Friday morning

The next morning, we woke up ready to hit The Yard. I was eager to see what new and upcoming acts they would feature this year, and of course the headliner. The Deltas, AKAs, and several other sororities and fraternities were out in full force, throwing up their signs. Gogo music blasted from the speakers, and the street was crammed with young men and women scoping out prospects. Most of these students were several years younger than us, so I wasn't trying to pick anything up, not to mention I was still reeling over my situation with Terrence. I just wanted to have a good time, feel the vibes, and hopefully connect with a few of my old classmates. Monique was ready, though. She had a face full of makeup plus too-tight jeans and a top that had way too much cleavage. Jamie and I reminded her it was chilly outside. She didn't care, though, because she was on the prowl.

"That's what jackets are for," she said.

We stayed on The Yard for several hours, laughing, dancing, enjoying the music, and catching up with the few school mates we did see. As usual, Jamie had several young men circling around us like sharks ready to attack, and Monique and I laughed as she shooed them away. Monique's oversized booty was literally bringing all the boys to The Yard, as Kelis would say, and I was … well, I was just vibin' and enjoying the festivities.

Right before we got ready to leave, Monique announced she had to make a quick bathroom run and sashayed off as Jamie and I stood reminiscing about some of the previous Homecomings we'd been to when we were actual students. It was amazing to see how time had flown, and we laughed about how we came from being lost freshwomen to now working in our careers.

Jamie said, "Look at us now, beautiful and successful, doing what we love."

I mulled over her statement, but I wasn't in agreement. I didn't feel successful, I damn sure didn't feel beautiful, and I wasn't sure if I even enjoyed being an attorney anymore. My mind was a million miles away when I heard a voice behind me.

"Anisa?"

I couldn't believe my ears, but I knew I'd heard right because I'd recognize that baritone anywhere. When I turned around, I stared straight into the face of a blast from the past. It took me five seconds to take all of him in. He looked older, but in a good way. He had a goatee and shoulder-length dreads. His arms were muscular, and I could tell there was no bird to be found on his chest. This was a grown man right here.

"Zahair?" I blinked a few times to make sure I was seeing correctly. Even with the extra clothing on to hide my extra baggage—if you will—I became self-conscious right away. I was never a small woman, but I was at least fifty pounds heavier than when I was in college, and he was, well … he was perfect. He cheesed at me with his perfect white teeth, ran over to me, and effortlessly picked me up and spun me around.

"Wow, this is an unexpected surprise!" he exclaimed.

Oh, and he smelled damn good. I blushed.

"Wow, Zahair! What brings you here?" Duh! There I was saying dumb stuff again. Why wouldn't he be here? He attended this school, too.

He raised his eyebrows at me and smirked.

Zahair and I had met in my sophomore year and his junior one at one of the dorm parties that a mutual friend had invited me to at the Towers. We flirted some, but I didn't take him seriously. I knew what went down at these parties, and I was not that girl. I was still a nerdy virgin who had barely had more than a pop kiss in high school. I remember standing around, feeling out of place because when Jamie and I walked in, the men flocked to her. I was left standing there, pretending to feel confident as I danced in a corner of the room alone.

Zahair had spotted me and tried to run game. He was definitely scrawnier than I liked, but he was cute, had nice teeth, and he smelled good. Those three things were non-negotiables for me. He kissed my hand and told me how pretty he thought I was that night.

"Yeah right," I'd said. "You must think I'm dumb. All these girls in here and you want me?" *There's no way,* I thought.

"Who, them? These women don't have nothing on you." He shrugged and I blushed as Wiz Khalifa's "Black and Yellow" came on. Now I must say, not only could I sing, but I also knew how to move my ass, and this was my shit. I started moving my hips, and he kept right up with me.

I was always impressed with a man who could dance, so when Usher's "There Goes My Baby" began to play and Zahair backed me up in the corner and put his lips on mine, I didn't object. His lips were soft. I didn't know what I was doing, so I pulled my face away when he attempted to slip his tongue in my mouth. I'd waited for years to have my first real kiss, and I didn't know if I wanted it in the corner of some dingy dorm room, but when I opened my eyes and saw how his eyes glazed over as he stared at me, I let my guard down and let him go for it.

He leaned in for the second time and this time I opened my mouth and let his tongue dance with mine. It felt … good. I didn't have much to compare it to, but he seemed like a good kisser, so I let him do it again. Needless to say, we hung out for the rest of the night.

Before we left, he asked me for my phone number, and we began dating. We never got serious. Although he was patient with me, I wasn't ready to go all the way with him. Because of my insecurities, I eventually pushed him away and back into the dating pool. I didn't feel I could give him what he wanted.

He stayed in DC after he graduated, so we stayed in touch for a while, but once I graduated and went back home to Miami, our relationship eventually fizzled out. The last thing I heard was that he had messed around and gotten some chick pregnant.

I asked, "So, Zahair, are you here alone?" I did a quick glance at his finger to see if I saw any traces of a ring, but I saw none.

I was just waiting for him to tell me he was here with his wife, but he answered, "I'm here with my boy, Tyrone. You remember him, right?" and motioned with his thumb over his shoulder. I glanced over, and Tyrone waved. I did remember him. What a coincidence. He and Jamie messed around in college some like me and Zahair. He looked pretty much the same as well.

I waved back.

"And what about you? Who are you here with?" he asked.

I glanced around and spotted Jamie a few feet away, scrolling through her phone. *How did she get over there? She must've slipped away to give us some space.* I pointed in her direction. "Oh, my friend Jamie. You remember her, don't you?" I knew he would. I mean, what man wouldn't?

He glanced up for a brief moment "Sure," he replied casually but immediately returned his attention to me.

I did a quick scan of The Yard and added, "Oh, and my other friend Monique from Miami is here, too. She's around here somewhere."

"Cool," he said, but I realized he wasn't concerned with that. He got straight to the point. "So, are you married? Any kids?"

No, but I might get pregnant tonight. "No, unfortunately not."

"Oh, really? I'm surprised someone didn't snatch you up by now."

Shit, you can snatch me up at any time. "Yeah, it's not easy out here, *and* I'm going to be thirty next month."

"Girl, you don't look a day over twenty-two," he said, laughing.

Okay, now he was going too far. "Zahair, you're too kind," I said, blushing. "So anyway, what about you? Are you married? Any kids?"

"I was married, briefly, to the mother of my child. It wasn't a good situation, and we divorced several years ago. I've been enjoying the single life ever since."

Yes! Yes! Yes! "Oh, I'm so sorry to hear it didn't work out. Oh, and I didn't know you had kids," I lied.

"Yeah? Really?" he asked as he excitedly whipped out his phone to show his mini-me's picture. "He just turned eight."

"Wow! He looks just like you. He's adorable," I gushed.

He nodded his agreement and beamed with pride as he glanced at the photo. "Thanks. Yeah, that's my little man right there."

He put his phone back in his pocket. "So, are you still living in Miami?"

"Yep."

"Okay, well how long do you plan to be here?"

As long as you'd like. "Umm, only 'til Monday afternoon. We've been here since Wednesday."

"Dang, I wish I would've known. We could've hung out."

Oh, we can definitely make up for lost time. "Yeah, me too. We still have the weekend, though."

"Yeah." He nodded. "That's true."

A moment of awkward silence engulfed us before he finally asked, "Well, do you mind if I have your number?"

Hell nah, I don't mind! "Okay," I answered. He saved my number and called my phone to make sure I had his.

He said, "I'll check you later this evening to see if you're free."

"Okay, cool. See you later."

He strolled off and I made my way over to Jamie and Monique, who were cheesing like they'd lost the sense God gave them.

Monique teased, "We saw you over there looking all cozy," and the three of us giggled.

I tried to ignore the butterflies in my gut. "Girl, I'm not here for all that. I just want to have a good time and take my ass home."

They rolled their eyes.

Jamie added, "Not with all that chemistry I just saw. Girl, please, you need to just go with the flow."

I asked, "Speaking of going with the flow, Jamie, did you see Tyrone?"

It didn't take her long to figure out who I was talking about. Her eyes lit up. "Oh. Tyrone? Tyrone?" She looked around. "Where?"

Monique was lost. "Who the hell is Tyrone?"

"Just an old friend," Jamie answered, as she continued to scour the crowd. "We were never too serious, we just hung out."

"Mm-hmm. If you say so." I chuckled. Jamie might pretend she didn't care, but the look on her face said otherwise.

"Anyways," Monique added, throwing in her two cents. "I don't know about y'all, but I'm not limiting my options this weekend. I'm just saying."

I was scared shitless, but I agreed that this might not be the weekend to play it safe. Maybe this was the time to let my afro free.

CHAPTER 12

Check Yo' self Before You Wreck Yo' self

We decided to hit up Busboys and Poets at 14th and U to grab something to eat. As usual, there was a wait at this restaurant/bookstore, but that didn't sway us. Jamie and I loved this spot, and we couldn't come to DC and not hit them up. It was definitely a go-to for great food and even better ambiance, and I was dying to try their blackened salmon. We enjoyed a few cocktails, finished eating, and swung by a local Black-owned bookstore on Good Hope Road SE to peruse their book catalog. We made it our business to support Black-owned bookstores wherever possible because we needed them to stay in business. I was particularly interested in this new writer

Keisha WriteNow Allen from Miami. I added her name to my list of authors to check out.

I was excited about tonight. Hopefully I would hear from Zahair, and even better, get the chance to hang out with him. I welcomed the chance to find out more about his life and what he'd been doing throughout the years, and if our chemistry was anything like I felt out on The Yard, maybe we'd do a little more.

We rested up for about an hour and got ready for our show. I was overly excited to see DC's own Bela Dona perform that night, as my cousin was the keyboardist and they were an all-female band. *Thank God for Spanx,* I acknowledged as I studied myself in the mirror. I had decided to throw caution to the wind and wear the tightest jeans in my closet, and I found an off-the-shoulder top as well to set it off just right. *Not bad. No, fuck that, I'm looking good, dammit!* Jamie stepped in and did my makeup and even Monique cosigned my look—she was extremely hard to please. Zahair called as I was stepping into my pumps.

"Hello," I breathed in my sexiest voice.

His voice was smooth as silk. "Hello, Anisa."

Damn, he won. "How's it going, Zahair? What're you up to?"

"Oh, Tyrone and I are getting ready to grab some grub and then probably find a spot to head out to."

"Oh. Okay. We're headed out now to catch Bela Dona if you wanted to join us. You can get the tickets online."

"Hmm." He paused in contemplation. "Those are some bad girls. I might just take you up on that."

"If not, maybe you and I can meet up afterwards," I blurted out before I realized what I was saying. Shit! Shit! Shit! I wasn't ready. If we were together in public, I was safe, but I knew if he got me alone, I couldn't be held responsible for my actions.

"Definitely!" he agreed. "I'll text you later to let you know if we can make it to the show, but if not, we'll figure it out because I want to see you tonight."

"Sounds good," I replied, and I knew my ass had just written a check I wasn't sure I was ready to cash.

When we got to the spot, it was crowded, and I was glad this wasn't an event where we would have to stand up all night because my feet were already killing me. We found our seats and Monique—being Monique—scoured the room for prospects.

"Girl, it's some niceness up in here!" she exclaimed. She motioned to a brother who was leaning up against the wall and fanned herself. "Look at him. Damn. Good God!"

"Good God is right!" I stated.

Jamie checked him out as well. "Yeah," Jamie agreed, "he's definitely looking right."

"I should go say something," Monique declared.

Jamie rolled her eyes. "Girl, you don't even know if he's here alone."

"You're right, but closed mouths don't get fed, so I'm about to find out. I'm trying to get me a little DC dick before I go back. Be right back." And with that, she sauntered off.

Jamie and I died with laughter, but my girl was not playing. She sashayed her way over to Mr. Damn-Good-God.

We laughed some more, and Jamie shook her head. "Girl, Mo's a mess, but she gets hers." She paused. "By the way, did you hear back from Zahair?"

I let her know I'd mentioned the show to him, and he said he would see if he could make it, but if not, he definitely planned to see me later.

"Sounds like you might be getting you some, too," she teased.

I wanted to, but I still wasn't fully convinced. "I don't know, Jamie. I'm still dealing with this stuff from Terrence."

She elbowed me. "Look, I'm not telling you to fall in love. I'm just saying, enjoy yourself! I mean, isn't that what you came here to do?"

I pondered her question. "Yeah, but we have a history. What if I end up feeling something?"

She rolled her eyes again. "Chile, we only get to do this thing called life once. Enjoy him, and if you feel something, hey. You deal with it then, but you're grown."

I paused. "Wait, look who's talking. I haven't seen you with any male counterparts lately."

"Listen," she replied. "Don't think I'm not getting it in here and there. I'm definitely open to the possibilities if the right man comes along, especially now that my career is slowing down some." She pointed both index fingers to herself, saying, "I can't let all this goodness go to waste."

We laughed again and slapped five when we heard the band begin to play.

Monique sat down cheesing and held up a business card as she mouthed, "Got it!"

We laughed some more. Only Mo.

It didn't take us long to get up out of our seats as Bela Dona showed out. When I couldn't take the pain from my pinkie toe being squeezed in my pumps anymore, I kicked them off. We danced until I felt sweat beads forming under my armpits and forehead, but I didn't care. They infused some of everything with gogo: Chaka Khan, Beyoncé, H.E.R, Rihanna, and too many other artists to name. I was in awe of how they seamlessly made those melodies come together.

While the show was going on, Zahair texted me to let me know he wouldn't be able to make it, but we were definitely still on for later that night. I smiled because as small as it seemed, at the least, it appeared that he could keep his word.

While I was greeting my cousin in the band and congratulating her on a wonderful show, Zahair called.

My heartbeat sped up as I answered with sweaty palms. "Hello," I said as I walked away from the crowd so I could hear him better.

"Hey. Are you still at the show?"

"Yeah, it just ended. We're getting ready to leave shortly."

"Okay. Tyrone and I actually aren't staying too far from there. I can drop him off and meet you where you're staying, if you'd like?"

"Umm, is Tyrone single?"

"Yep."

"No, bring him along. I'll send you the address and you can meet us there."

"Okay, see you soon."

I chuckled. We were all going to enjoy some male company tonight, one way or the other. We ended the call, and in that moment, I made my mind up to go with the flow for the rest of this trip, whatever that might be.

CHAPTER 13

It Ain't No Fun if My Homies Can't Get None

"You did what?" Jamie asked incredulously as she drove us back to our Airbnb.

I shrugged. "I told Zahair to bring Tyrone."

"Why would you do that?" she asked.

Monique and I fell out with laughter as Jamie had a hissy fit. "Go with the flow, remember?" I reminded her.

"Ugh, really, Anisa? You ain't right!" But it didn't take her long to back down and join in. "Well, how did he look?"

"Good. Pretty much the same as college days."

Monique had already confirmed she would be meeting up with her newfound friend tonight, so we could do whatever we wanted to. Good ol' Monique. I wished I could be as confident and bold as she was.

We got back to the Airbnb and got ready for Zahair and Tyrone to come through. Jamie and I suggested we all sit out in the living room where we could all vibe and have a little wine without feeling pressured. I liked that idea, but when Zahair and Tyrone showed up, I wasn't sure how long that would last, because Zahair was looking pretty damn tasty. From the way Jamie's face lit up when she saw Tyrone, it didn't look like she'd be in the living room for long either.

We each sipped on our wine and sat around chatting until Monique announced that her date was outside and she was heading out. We made her give us his name, phone number, and license plate number just in case we needed to come out and wreck shop, but we were quite sure if he did anything Monique didn't like, he was the one who'd be having issues.

It was getting late, and Zahair and I were vibin' so well that I didn't realize the time, especially after a few glasses of wine.

I let him know that I was an attorney and a new homeowner, and he was fascinated to know that I could sing as well.

"One day, I hope to hear you sing," he added.

I pretended not to hear him and kept on talking.

We spent our time reminiscing, and I found out that he was a realtor and poet, lived in Petworth, wanted to get married again (to the right woman, of course), and wanted at least one more child. His likes: hip hop, jazz, and soul music; fragrance body oil rolls; natural women; people that thought outside of the box; traveling; and cooking. His dislikes: liars, bad communicators, bad hygiene, big weddings, and bouquet and garter tosses. When I asked him what his issue was with big weddings, he replied, "People just spend too much money on weddings. I don't agree with it. They spend all that money and then get divorced a year later. You want to know why?" he asked.

Before I could answer, he continued, "I'll tell you why. Because they concentrate more on the wedding and not on the marriage. That's why."

I nodded my head, but he wasn't done.

"And we all know that the whole bouquet and garter toss thing is a big myth. I haven't met anyone who got married after catching any of them. It's just corny."

I decided to leave that part alone.

He was deep, though, and his insight on life was amazing. I didn't realize how much of a free spirit he was. I didn't remember him being this way in college. I remembered him being intelligent, but this man before me was quite intriguing.

Talking to Zahair was effortless. It was almost like we picked up right where we left off in college. The main difference was that this time I wasn't a virgin.

After a while, always the gentleman, Zahair asked if I was ready for him to leave, and I knew it was now or never.

"I'm good," I informed him. "It's been awesome catching up with you, and I'm glad that we bumped into each other today."

He cheesed. "Me too, Anisa. This has been … really nice."

I was unsure of a lot in my life at that time, but in that moment, the one thing I knew without a doubt was that I didn't want him to go tonight. He was bringing out all kinds of emotions in me, and honestly, it felt good. *Besides, this is just sex between two old friends,* I told myself. Just a temporary distraction, I reasoned, but I had no clue what I was about to get myself into.

We announced we were going in for the night and I saw the all-knowing look on Jamie's face. I could tell she was happy I was living in the moment for once. When we got back to my room, I felt as if I were transported back to when we were in college; I felt the butterflies in my stomach, only this time I knew I'd finally be sampling what I was missing back then.

"Give me a second, and make yourself at home," I told him as I went off to the bathroom. I studied myself in the mirror and ordered myself silently to *just breathe, girl. Live in the moment and enjoy yourself.*

I undressed and stared at my body as Terrence's words echoed in my head: *Look at you. No one is ever going to want you.*

I wrestled with that for a moment until I remembered my daddy's words: *You know better than to let this punk keep you down. Don't ever let anyone steal your shine.*

"Thanks, Daddy," I whispered and pulled my robe on and stepped out into the bedroom.

When Zahair saw me, his eyes lit up and his eyebrows rose.

"Damn, girl!" he exclaimed. His phone was on the dresser and Raheem DeVaughn was singing "You."

Hell, he wasn't looking too bad over there with his sexy self.

I'd made sure to keep on my undergarments because I wanted him to work a little, not to mention the lights were still on.

He got up and strolled over to me. When he got to me, he gazed into my eyes, slid his hands into my robe's opening and rasped, "I've wanted you for a long time." His hands slowly caressed my body as I closed my eyes.

That caught me off guard because I figured a man as good looking as Zahair had unlimited options when it came to women. *You don't have to wait any longer with your sexy ass,* I thought. "Well, here I am," I whispered.

He leaned down and kissed me, and I felt every nerve ending in my body begin to tingle. Surprisingly, our chemistry was still strong as ever. He walked me backward to the bed as our tongues danced, and I realized Terrence had nothing on Zahair's kissing skills. He opened my robe and stepped back a little while holding it open. He tilted his head. I felt self-conscious again.

I said, "Wait, hold on one sec," as I reached over to turn off the lights, but he was quick. He grabbed my wrist gently.

"What're you doing?" he asked.

"Oh, I'm just turning off the lights," I replied nervously.

"No, Anisa, I want to see you."

"But I—" I began, but he put his mouth on mine again and silenced me with a kiss.

My body felt warm all over as he slid my robe off and let it drop to the floor, then he stepped back a second time to take me in again.

My hands instinctively went up over my midsection as I tried to cover what I thought were my imperfections.

"Mm-hmm," he said and gently removed my hands. He nodded his approval and stared at me when he said, "Anisa, your body is amazing."

I was still feeling self-conscious when he came back over to me and gently kissed the nape of my neck while reaching behind me and simultaneously unsnapping my bra. Damn, he was smooth!

He stepped back a third time to take more of me in. He was sending my mind into a tailspin while I fought to keep it together. Never had anyone looked at me the way he did. He stared at me while pulling his shirt over his head, then he unbuckled his jeans and stepped out of them and stood in front of me in nothing but his boxer briefs as his huge bulge beckoned to me.

"Damn," I breathed. Just as I'd thought, his chest and arms were defined and sculpted. I stood there, mesmerized by his toned physique.

He came to me and put his mouth on my neck and shoulders. Before I could say anything, he got on his knees and began to pull my panties down. His face was right in front of my womanhood and I froze as I realized what he was about to do. It had been so long since anyone had put their mouth on me in this way that I didn't know what to do with myself. He lifted my right leg and slung it over his shoulder as his fingers began to probe. I felt my leg trembling as he opened me up like a flower and put his warm mouth on me.

"Oh my God!" I moaned. All of this and I didn't have to ask, suggest, or beg? This man was blowing my mind.

My left leg began to quiver, and he grabbed my ass and leg that was on his shoulder and held me firmer. I stared down at him with my mouth open, and he stared up at me as he licked my clit so good tears began to form in my eyes. I put my hands in his dreads to steady myself because I felt like I was going to pass out.

"I got you, baby," he rasped and stared up at me.

When I thought I couldn't take it anymore, he took my leg down and stood up slowly.

He grabbed my hand and pulled me toward the bed. I got in first as he watched me. When I grabbed the covers as another way to cover my nakedness, he moved them away.

"Lay down, queen," he ordered gently.

"Wh-what?" I stammered.

"Just relax," he said as he stared down at me. He reached over on the dresser for what appeared to be baby oil. I hadn't seen that there before, so he must've brought it with him.

He straddled me as he gazed down at me and poured the oil into his open palm. When his hands made contact with my neck and shoulders, I felt a warm sensation.

I moaned as he slowly massaged my neck and shoulders. He then had me turn over as he massaged my back. Never had a man taken this much care and time in appreciating my body. It felt like I was in a dream.

When he was done rubbing me all over, he began running kisses up and down my spine. Everywhere his mouth touched, my body tingled. I wasn't sure if it was the oil or just his amazing mouth, but whatever it was, I was in love.

When he was done, he had me turn back over, and he put his mouth on my breasts and gently bit my nipples as I moaned again. He ran kisses down my stomach and went back down below again. Syleena Johnson's "Slowly" clicked on as he licked and sucked until my eyes rolled back and I began to run away from him, but his strong arms held my legs tight so I couldn't move.

"Ahhhh!" I shouted. Thank goodness he had the music playing loudly from his phone to drown out my screams from the immeasurable pleasure he was causing. Shortly after, my body convulsed. He kept going as I climaxed over and over, and my clit was tender, and I had to beg him to stop. I'd heard stories about this, but I'd never been brought to climax this way.

He came back up and stared at me, asking, "You sure? You know I could do this to you all night."

My eyes widened. I never thought that I could *not* want to be pleasured orally. How I went from forgetting what it felt like to having too much in just one night was blowing my mind. I was ready to give him all my cookies and couldn't take it anymore.

"I need you," I whispered. He retrieved his condom from the dresser and looked me in the eyes as he slowly entered me. He stretched me to full capacity as I closed my eyes. He moved slowly at first and then began to pick up the pace as his hip movements sent me over the edge.

He said, "Look at me."

I opened my eyes briefly, but as another orgasm began to rip through me, I squeezed them shut again.

"Oh. My. God. I'm. Cuming!" I shouted.

"Open your eyes. I want to see your eyes," he commanded.

So, I did. He bit his bottom lip and his eyes glazed over as he watched me, and when my eyes grew wide, he softly ordered, "Come for me again, Anisa." And that's just what I did as my body shuddered and tears formed in my eyes.

Shortly after, he closed his eyes, sped his hips up, and shouted through clenched teeth, "Damn, baby. Shiiit!" as he finally let go.

When we were done, we basked in our afterglow and he whispered, "Anisa, you're a queen, and don't you ever forget that." For the first time in a while, I actually believed it. He had me open, mentally and physically.

I'd never seen such restraint, care, and strength at the same time. In that moment, I realized this was the first time I'd ever been fully naked on all levels, with any man.

CHAPTER 14

Don't Wake Me Because I Must be Dreamin'

I had to pinch myself because I felt this might have all been a dream, but when I opened my eyes the next morning and looked over and he was still beside me, I said a silent prayer of thanks. Zahair was asleep on his back and his dreads were laid out on the pillow. His dark skin reminded me of an African prince, or perhaps Black Jesus, because he damn sure had me calling on God last night.

When he opened his eyes and caught me staring at him, he rubbed his eyes, stretched, and smiled. "Good morning, my queen." Damn, even with crust in his eyes, he was still gorgeous.

I blushed. "Good morning, yourself," I answered.

I caught how he was staking claim to me by calling me "his" queen, and even if he wasn't serious, it felt good.

I wanted to jump his bones, but what I didn't want was to fall in love for what he could do for me in the bedroom, especially when I would be leaving in the next few days.

He yawned, stretched again, and propped himself up on the pillow with his elbow and asked, "What are you planning to do today?"

Hopefully you. "Well, we're going to head out to the Reggae Wine and Food Festival today in Mount Airy. You know we don't miss anything to do with wine."

He chuckled. "I know."

I decided not to invite him right away because although I had an amazing night, I didn't know if Jamie and Monique could say the same thing. But when I got up to go to the living room and heard Jamie humming "He Loves Me" by Jill Scott, I reconsidered.

"Anyone heard from Monique?" I asked, but when she strolled in with the bun that she had meticulously positioned on top of her head the day before leaning to the side, I figured we all had a good night.

"So, are we going to Linganore with just the ladies today?" I asked. We all looked at each other.

"Nah," we agreed in unison.

We all spent much of the day at the wine festival, and Zahair grinded on me as we laughed and danced for most of our time there. We came back to the Airbnb to shower, rest, and change for our next spot. The gentlemen joined us for much of the rest of the weekend, and I was glad Monique and I had decided to take Monday off so we could squeeze more activities in. We hit up a '90s party that night at Society Lounge, and we danced until I felt the sweat running down my back, and then we got some brunch the next morning, did some touring during the day, and then went to the Howard Theatre the next evening to see a local artist perform.

Everywhere we went, Zahair would grab my hand, and he held on to me like his life depended on it. Even with an occasional glance at other women, he never made me feel that I didn't have his full attention. I felt like I was floating on a cloud any time I was in his presence. When we weren't out, we turned the room upside down with our sexual escapades, and just as I feared, I was feeling things for this man that I didn't think were possible.

Before I knew it, our fabulous weekend was over. That Sunday night, Zahair looked me in my eyes and said, "Anisa, I don't want this to end. I haven't felt this way about anyone in a long time, and I hope that we can continue to see each other."

Although it scared me, I felt the same way, but I couldn't allow myself to say that. Suppose I told him how I truly felt and then he found someone else? We didn't live in the same city, so I figured he probably had a bunch of women that he was talking to, and I didn't want to risk him choosing someone else over me. I wasn't willing to feel the pain of being rejected again.

I simply responded, "Yes, Zahair, this weekend has truly been special. I will cherish it forever."

"Well, let's see where this goes. I'm willing to travel if you don't mind doing the same."

I nodded and answered reluctantly, "I'd like that."

I was sad to be leaving his wonderfulness, but we both knew the situation before we jumped in. What neither of us realized at that moment, though, was that neither of us was a fan of long-distance relationships.

Before I went home, I decided to swing by Iya's place to see her and update her on my weekend. When she opened the door, the scent of her essential oils greeted me, and her beautiful face lit up as she squeezed me like she hadn't seen me in years.

In the usual fashion, her jazz music was playing, her head was tied with a beautiful scarf, and she was dressed like she had just come straight from the motherland. The only lights on in the house came from several of her lava lamps, and she had a glass of wine in her hand.

"Come in, queen!" she answered flamboyantly as she waved me in.

"How are you, Iya?" I smiled at her.

"I'm good, queen," she said, grinning. I followed her as she made her way to the kitchen, grabbed a glass, and poured me a glass of wine. She handed it to me, made her way to the couch, and patted the space beside her. "So, how was DC?"

I gave her a quick rundown of my trip, minus the Zahair part. "I had an awesome time," I added.

"Did you meet anyone?"

Damn, is she reading my astrology? I can't hide anything from her. "Well, I bumped into someone from college, and I'm really feeling him, Iya."

Her eyes widened and she applauded. "Ohhh, yes! Tell me more!"

I gave her the brief rundown about Zahair, minus all the sex we had.

When I was done, she exclaimed, "See, this is what I was trying to tell you. I'm glad you're opening yourself to the possibilities of meeting other men."

Yeah, that's not all that was open this weekend. "Yes, we had an amazing time. It was really good seeing him after all those years."

"Well, see, it's just the beginning. Doesn't it feel good to be free and to not be tied down to someone who isn't emotionally available to you?"

"Yes," I agreed.

We chatted some more over our wine and I reluctantly let her know that I had to leave so I could get ready for work the next day.

She walked me to the door, but before she closed it, she said,"Peace and blessings, queen. And Anisa?"

"Yes, Iya?"

"You're absolutely glowing. Any man that can make you glow like that is someone you should consider keeping around. I love you."

I blushed. "I love you, too."

CHAPTER 15

Sharing is Caring

On my drive home, I dialed Talia.

"Hey, Anisa!" she answered on the second ring. I hadn't heard her this excited to hear from me in quite some time.

"Hey, Lia!" I exclaimed.

"So how was DC?" Before she had gotten married and had Aaliyah, she had taken several trips to see and hang out with me, so she knew how they got down at Homecoming.

"Well, I'm fine," I teased.

"Sorry, sis, I'm just excited to hear about your trip."

"Do you remember Zahair?"

"Zahair … Zahair?" She paused and I could tell the

wheels were turning. "Oh yeah! The guy you were really into when you were at Howard. What about him?"

"Well, I bumped into him on The Yard. We hung out for most of the weekend."

"Ohhh, really?" she asked excitedly. "Well, how did he look?"

"Girl, he is a full-grown man in every sense of the word, not to mention smart as hell."

"Ohhh, so you got you some?" She laughed. "I'm glad to see you didn't let breaking up with Terrence stop you."

My sister knew me so well.

"Terrence who?" I laughed. I explained that Zahair had done things to me no other man had ever done. She was awestruck but ecstatic.

"See, I told you there were other men out there who you could be with who would make you forget about Terrence's ass."

"As usual, you were right," I answered.

She continued, "Oh, and I wanted to share something with you, but you have to promise that this stays between us."

I didn't have a problem with that because Talia and I shared secrets all the time. "Of course, what happened?"

"The other night, Nia shared with me that she's messing with a married man."

Oh, wow! I thought. I was over that situation. So basically, she and her husband were both two miserable cheaters. I wasn't perfect, but I could never condone that.

"Wow, why doesn't she just leave her husband if she's so unhappy?"

"I don't know, that's something you'd have to ask her."

"Yeah, I think I'm good on that."

She changed subjects. "Anyway, on a better note, someone's having their thirtieth birthday soon."

"Yeah. Don't remind me."

"Girl, why not? You should be celebrating your accomplishments and what you *do* have. That's more than enough to get excited about. You're a beautiful, successful attorney with money in the bank, and you have your own home. That's a lot more than a lot of thirty-year-olds can say."

"Yeah, I'm a single, fat attorney with no babies, too."

"Really, Nisa? There you go. Girl, I'm overweight, too, but these extra pounds ain't never stop no show, and Darius loves me and every one of these love handles. And since your weight is bothering you so much, what are you doing about it? Are you exercising? Have you changed your eating habits?"

"Not really."

"Well, Darius and I have started taking evening walks and I've started changing the way I prepare our food. I'd even begun losing a few pounds before I got pregnant. I didn't want to scare you, but before I got pregnant, my doctor let me know that I was pre-diabetic."

"Wow!" I replied. Her admission definitely caught me off guard. Nia was also pre-diabetic, so it wasn't a weight thing, it just ran in our family. "Well, I'm glad that you're doing what you have to do to take care of yourself because Aaliyah needs her mother."

"And we need you, too," she acknowledged, "so I hope you take better care of yourself as well."

I heard what she was saying, but she was acting like it was easy.

"Okay, sis. I hear you. I'll do better."

We finished speaking for the night, and I made a mental note to schedule my annual physical the next day.

The next morning, when I got to work, there was a stack of brand-new files piled up on my desk. I thumbed through some of them and just like I thought, they were either old or cases no one wanted to deal with. I was already annoyed. *You mean to tell me no one touched these things in over a week?* Typical. I grabbed several of the files and stormed off to Colin's office and knocked on his door.

"Come in!" he called. "Hey, Anisa," he exclaimed when I poked my head in. "Glad to see you're back. You're looking well."

I gave him the best plastic smile I could muster. "Thanks. Umm, Colin—"

"I hope you don't mind," he interrupted. "We got a little backed up, so we had to give everyone a little extra this month."

I didn't mind doing extra work, but some of these files were almost at their deadline. "Yes, but none of these files have been touched and some are several months old. Why were they just sitting on my desk? Suppose I'd been out a few more weeks?"

He paused. "I know it's a lot, but we're counting on you

to handle this. Make some calls and get the dates pushed back if you have to."

I could feel the steam coming out of my ears.

"Colin—"

"Or else, I'll get someone else to do it." He looked me firmly in the eyes.

Oh. I knew exactly what that meant. The jerk just threatened to fire me.

I opened my mouth to say something slick but thought better of it. "Yes, sir." I retreated. As I walked out of his office and headed down the hall, I caught a glimpse of Bill Turkey-Neck smirking. I wouldn't doubt that he had something to do with this.

I went to my office and worked until 7:00 p.m. sorting out my work and making calls. I packed up several files and took them home. For the next few weeks, my work consumed me, but I was determined not to let those assholes win. After a while, I didn't know if I was working this hard to prove I could do it for myself or just to prove them wrong.

CHAPTER 16

Thanks for Giving

A week before Thanksgiving, I was overjoyed when Zahair asked if I would mind if he came down and spent the weekend with me. There was no hesitation on my part because I knew he'd be an awesome distraction, not to mention I was missing him and was ready for some of that good good to help alleviate some of my stress.

He arrived on Friday evening. When he got in my car, he reminded me of a Black Adonis with his dreads pulled back and a little extra stubble on his face.

We stopped at Shuckin' & Jivin' and got some shrimp, macaroni and cheese, and collard greens before we headed back to my place. While we ate, we spoke about what had been going on with our lives since I'd gotten back.

"I've missed you," he confessed. "You've been so busy that we haven't spoken for more than a few minutes at a time. How are things going?"

I voiced my frustrations with feeling undervalued at my law office and how I didn't see myself growing there.

"Why don't you go to a new law office?" he asked.

"Zahair, I've been working there for three and a half years; I can't just up and leave. I've been working hard to show what I can do, and hopefully I can make partner one day. If I leave and go somewhere else, it'll be like starting over from scratch."

"Well, is it working? From what you've said, you feel undervalued and you haven't seen much growth. Personally, I think you can do better than a second-rate law office." He shrugged then mumbled, "I'm just saying, you don't seem happy there."

I heard what he was saying, and I knew I was an intelligent woman so I could definitely get hired somewhere else, but I didn't have enough confidence to try. Besides, this man was the epitome of Blackness, so I couldn't understand why he didn't understand my apprehension. I figured if anyone could understand the struggle, he would, so his question annoyed me. Furthermore, I didn't appreciate him calling my office low rate, even if it was true. "I'm a Black woman in corporate America. You know we have to work twice as hard as everyone else."

"I see," he said as he locked eyes with me, "but is this what you really want to do?"

"It's cool," I answered, "but I can't say it's something I want to do for the rest of my life."

"So, why are you going so hard to make someone else rich if you don't want to do it forever?"

Oh my goodness. He sounded just like my mother. I side-eyed him. "Because I spent years in law school busting my ass, and it pays the bills, Zahair."

"Okay ... okay!" He held his hands up and backed down. "Don't shoot the messenger."

He reached over me, grabbed the remote for the television, and clicked it on. "Oh, you have Pandora on here. Nice! Let's see what you got." He scrolled through my stations, clicked on H.E.R. radio, and "Best Part" came through my speakers.

"This is my shit!" he exclaimed. He grabbed my hands and pulled me up off the floor. We slow grinded all around my living room and when he put his lips on mine, I forgot I was aggravated with him just a few minutes before.

He pulled back and stared down at me. "Sing for me."

I was caught off guard. "What?"

"I said, I want you to sing for me."

I pulled away from him. "Zahair, you know I don't do that anymore."

He folded his arms and studied me. "And why is that?"

I sighed. I didn't want to tell him I was embarrassed because of my size; I knew he would find that unacceptable, and I honestly couldn't figure out why I cared so much about what he thought. I mean, he wasn't even my man, but he did have a way about him that made me want to open up.

I decided to oblige him. "Okay. Sing what?"

"Whatever your beautiful heart desires."

I thought about it for a few moments and Donny Hathaway's "A Song for You" came to mind. It was one of those songs Iya would sometimes let me close the show with. Sometimes when I was done, some of the audience would have tears in their eyes. I said, "Turn around."

"What?" he asked.

"I said turn around. If you want me to sing, I need you to turn around so you can't see me."

He chuckled but did as he was told.

I grabbed the remote for the television and hit the mute button, cleared my throat, and rolled my neck. My heart pounded, and my palms became sweaty. After my first few notes, my voice cracked. I stopped, found my center—as Iya would always tell me—took a deep breath, cleared my throat again, closed my eyes, and began to belt out the song. I sang every last word, over five minutes of the song, and when I was done, there were tears in my eyes.

Zahair didn't move for a moment, but when he finally turned around, I swear I saw him wipe his eyes.

When he finally found his voice, he shook his head and simply said, "Wow!"

"Wow what?"

"Just wow!" he answered. "I can't find the words, so I'll just leave it at that."

"Zahair!"

"Okay, okay. Listen, Anisa, people like you shouldn't be running from your gift. The way you sing is ... it's ... it's literally a gift from God! God gave you that gift so you could inspire and uplift others."

I blushed. What an awesome compliment. Dang, this man knew how to make me feel special without even trying. "Thanks, Zahair. You're sweet. I appreciate you for saying that."

He came over to me and grabbed my hands. "No, Anisa, I don't think you understand. I'm not just saying that. I'm declaring it! I wasn't just trying to give a compliment. I'm telling you now that you have to do what you were called to do or you'll never truly be happy."

Before I could object, he put his lips on mine again and kissed any doubt I had away. This time his kisses were more urgent than they'd been before, and I followed his lead. He lifted my dress over my head and dropped it on the floor. He sat on the couch, grabbed my hands, and pulled me onto his lap. He pulled my face down gently and kissed me deeply. He freed my breasts from my bra one by one and put his mouth everywhere his hands touched. I remembered the lights were on but didn't try to reach for the lamp to switch them off this time. He let me ride him right there on that couch until my legs shook and my body tingled, and then he laid me down and made love to me. In that moment, I felt like the prettiest girl in the world.

CHAPTER 17

The Devil is a Liar

That morning, as we slept, my phone rang. I cursed and glanced up at my nightstand. The clock read 7:00 a.m. I silenced my phone without looking up. It rang again a few minutes later. I glanced over and the name *Terrence* flashed across my screen. I blinked a few times and rubbed my eyes to see if I'd seen correctly, but the name didn't change. *Oh no, he didn't,* I thought. I silenced it once more. I heard my phone ding to signal that he'd left a message and the screen showed I had a text. I hit the button to read it. The text read, "Anisa, I need to talk to you. It's about my son."

At first, I was upset he would have the nerve to call me, but then I realized that although I wanted to hate Terrence,

I still cared about him. I decided to see what was up. I sat up and looked down at Zahair as he stirred, but he didn't open his eyes, so I got up and walked out to the living room so I could call Terrence back.

My stomach did flip-flops as I hit the redial button. Why I still cared was beyond me. Terrence answered on the first ring.

"Hey, Anisa! It's so good to hear your voice."

I leaned against the wall and shifted my weight from one leg to the other. He sounded good. Really good.

Mm-hmm, how's your eye? "What do you want, Terrence?" I hoped I didn't sound angry because I didn't want him to think I still cared.

He sighed. "Mikel and his mother were in a car accident last night."

All of my anger quickly turned to worry. "Oh my God!" I exclaimed. "Are they okay?"

"Yes, yes, yes," he assured me. "We're at the hospital now. Asha broke her wrist and is pretty banged up, and Mikel escaped with just a couple of minor bruises, thank God."

"Oh, thank God," I breathed. I pressed my hand to my chest, and I realized my heart was racing.

"Thanks, Anisa. I mean … thanks for caring."

We sat on the phone for a few moments in awkward silence. I finally spoke. "Okay, Terrence. Well, you take care of yourself."

He shouted before I could hang up, "Anisa!"

I sighed. "Yes, Terrence?"

"I never stopped loving you, and I miss you."

"Terrence, I—"

"And I want you back."

I stared at the phone in amazement as Zahair emerged from the bedroom, stretching.

"I gotta go," I replied and hung up.

Zahair yawned and stretched again before he spoke. "Hey, there. I heard you on the phone. Is everything okay?"

"Umm, sure. That was an old friend."

"Okay."

I hated that I lied to Zahair, but at that moment, I was taken off guard. Had I just heard Terrence say he wanted me back? I was feeling stuck on stupid. Why should I even entertain anything he said to me? The words, *Look at you. No one is ever going to want you,* had cut me like a knife and haunted me since that day. Those words transported me back to the first grade and reminded me of being rejected because of my weight time and time again, so I'd be a fool to ever talk to him again. Right? Besides, now I had Zahair in my life.

The one thing I did know was that Terrence and I had history, and when things were good, they were good, but the bad was really bad. But didn't every relationship have its ups and downs? And what about him and Asha? Maybe he realized I was the one for him after all?

I offered Zahair breakfast. "Hey, would you like some grits, bacon, eggs, and biscuits?"

He rubbed his washboard stomach and flashed his gorgeous smile. "Sure, that sounds delicious. Woman, you're going to make me gain weight. Would you like some help?"

I wanted him beside me as much as possible but figured

I could use some time to gather my thoughts while I cooked. "I got it, handsome." I winked.

I put SiR on shuffle and let him sing to me as I prepared breakfast. Unfortunately, the time I spent in the kitchen only gave me more time to think, adding to my anxiety.

Over our delicious breakfast, if I do say so myself, Zahair caught me off guard. "Would you be open to relocating?" he asked.

I damn-near choked on my biscuit. "Relocating where?" I asked as I took a sip of orange juice.

"DC," he answered matter-of-factly.

"Oh—I, umm." I didn't expect this question so soon, especially because just last night I told him how I was trying to make a name for myself at my company. "Why do you ask?"

"Anisa, I like what we're building here, and I figure that sooner or later, one of us is going to have to relocate if we keep going like this."

I was shocked at his candor. I put it back on him. "Well, what about you?" I asked. "Would you consider relocating?"

He looked up as he pondered my question. He shrugged. "I would actually think about it if my son wasn't there, but I don't want to leave until he's at least eighteen."

I had forgotten about that. Damn. "Remember what I told you about building a name for myself at my law firm? Plus, I have a home, and my whole family is here," I countered.

"I see. Well, I could support you financially while you searched for another company to work for, and you could rent your home out. And what about pursuing a singing career? I know several people that could help you out, and New York isn't that far if you needed to go back and forth."

I didn't need anyone to help me financially because one of the things that I did well was stack my money. I'd spent plenty of time doing my research on the best ways to grow generational wealth. I knew how important that was since I was planning to have a family one day. I'd purchased real estate and started saving and investing in stocks years before. I had a diversified portfolio.

"I have money saved, so that's not an issue," I pointed out. I wasn't sure how I felt about him putting this kind of pressure on me. I paused because I wanted to make sure I phrased my next point correctly. At that moment, I made up every excuse as to why I couldn't have a singing career. "*You* said I should pursue a singing career, though. I never agreed that's what I was going to do. Besides, I'm almost thirty. Don't you think I'm a little too old to just be starting a singing career?"

He wasn't trying to hear it. He leaned forward so he could make sure he had my full attention. "Are you serious, Anisa? Thirty is not old, so I don't know where you're getting that from, and the tears in your eyes after you belted out that song last night said that's what you *need* to be doing." He paused and leaned back. "And besides, who says you can't do both music and law?"

I shook my head and went back to eating. I couldn't deny I'd felt something when I opened my mouth the night before. I was transported to another space; it was almost as if I'd had an out-of-body experience in that moment. It was a spiritual encounter that was beyond description, and you would've had to be in the moment to understand it.

Even so, I was too afraid of the unknown. I already had a blueprint for my life, and I planned on sticking to it.

He said, "So, tell me something. Am I wasting my time here?"

I shrugged and stared down at my plate.

"Anisa—"

"Zahair, I don't want to talk about this anymore. This matter is closed."

He shook his head then opened his mouth to say something, but he thought better of it and we finished our meal in silence. When he was done, he wiped his mouth with his napkin and said, "Anisa, I want someone I can build with, but you don't seem ready. I wouldn't have flown all the way out here if I didn't want to explore that."

I heard what he said, but I wasn't ready to accept it. Maybe things were moving too fast with him, and I was afraid. Maybe I felt he was too good to be true or maybe just too good for me. I didn't look up when I said, "I don't know what to tell you."

We sat in silence for what felt like some of the longest moments of my life. Eventually, he replied, "I can't love you more than *you* love you, and I damn sure can't be more interested in your happiness than you are." With that, he got up from the table and left the room just as SiR's "You Can't Save Me" clicked on. Go figure.

He loves me? Did Zahair just say he loves me? I grappled with all that had just happened within the last few hours of my life. I had two men tell me they loved me that day, when it took me almost thirty years to barely even get one man to say it.

What the hell was going on? The universe sure had a funny sense of humor.

CHAPTER 18

Oh, Hell Nah!

"You did what?" Jamie and Monique asked in unison. I had picked up some chicken and waffles from NoMi Bar and Grill after I dropped Zahair off at the airport the next afternoon, and I needed an outlet after all that had gone on that weekend.

The rest of my weekend with Zahair was pretty uneventful for the most part. He was still a gentleman and he hadn't mentioned what we spoke about again, but the passion wasn't in his eyes like before I told him I probably wouldn't ever be relocating. We had taken a ride out to Wynwood on Saturday, walked around for a while, gone to a Black-owned book store in West Palm Beach to get some books to add to my collection, and then watched *13th*, *She Did That*, and some other thought-provoking documentaries on Netflix for the rest of his time in Miami. I could admit I was falling—no, I *fell* for him as well—but he was ten steps ahead of me. I'd be a fool to pick up my whole life and follow a man after what I'd just gone through with Terrence.

I hadn't mentioned that Zahair was coming to anyone because I knew my mother, Nia, and Talia would've conveniently found a way to meet him, and I wasn't ready for all of that yet. I was especially glad I hadn't done that after I'd gotten that call from Terrence. I hadn't heard back from him since that day, but I planned at the least to send him a text to see if his son had been discharged from the hospital.

I repeated myself to answer Jamie and Monique. "I told him I didn't see myself relocating."

Monique: "Ever? I mean, look, I get it, and I'd miss you, but you won't even entertain the idea of moving one day? I mean, you love DC, and you keep telling me how wonderful this man is. And besides, it's not like you have anything special going on here."

Jamie: "Yeah, I saw the way you looked at him when we were in DC. Plus, I'd only be a few hours away if you needed me."

Me: "Well, I have my home, and I *do* have a career."

I changed subjects.

"Another thing—he also kept insisting that I make singing into a career."

Monique: "And? What's so wrong with that? You can blow, and you've mentioned to me on several occasions that you know you have the pipes but just wish you had the confidence to back it up."

Jamie: "Yeah, you have been saying that as long as I've known you. And who said you can't be a musician *and* a lawyer?"

Me: "Dang, Jamie, you sound just like him. I can't just up and make a career change at thirty."

Jamie: "Why the hell not? People do it all the time. Anyways, it's just something to think about."

Me: "I guess … I hear you."

I took a deep breath and changed subjects a second time. "So, another thing. Terrence called."

As expected, Monique was not pleased, and it didn't take her long to let me know it.

Monique: "Oh, hell nah. Is he the real reason you said you wouldn't move to DC? What did his sorry ass want?"

Jamie: "Oh really? What's up with him?"

Me: "No, Monique, and his son and baby's mom were in a car accident."

Jamie: "Oh no! Are they okay?"

Monique: "Umph. Anybody die?"

Me: "Thank goodness, they're both okay. Asha broke her wrist and is pretty banged up, but Mikel just had a few cuts and bruises."

Jamie: "Thank God!"

Monique: "Good. Now that you know they're okay, there's no need to talk to his trifling ass again."

I sighed. "I don't know. I'll probably send him a text, at least, to see if they're out of the hospital."

Jamie: "Oh, okay. That's nice of you."

Monique: "What the fuck for? Didn't he say they were fine?"

I rolled my eyes. "It's called courtesy, Mo."

Monique: "Girl, bye. He wasn't too courteous when he told you no one would want your ass."

I got silent because I couldn't be mad at her for feeling that way. He had messed me up mentally, and they were the ones picking up the pieces afterwards, but two wrongs didn't make a right and I missed him. Three years was a long time, and I did love him.

Thankfully, Monique changed the subject.

Monique: "Well, anyway, I'm excited to hang out for your birthday next weekend."

Jamie: "Yeah, I'll be flying in on Thursday evening."

For my birthday, we were going to see Iya perform at Lorna's and then head out to do a little late-night partying afterwards. I didn't plan to do anything as I didn't feel that festive, but my friends and family insisted.

"You only turn thirty once," they'd said.

When the ladies and I hung up, Ole Faithful decided to text Terrence to follow up on how his son was doing.

He called me immediately. "Hey, you," he said casually.

"Hey, Terrence. I was just checking to see if Mikel and Asha had been discharged?"

"Yes, they both came out today. You don't know how happy it makes me that you would take the time to call … to check on them, that is."

Well, I was really only checking on Mikel, but I would've

been wrong if I didn't ask about both of them. "Yes, of course," I answered.

"That's one of the things I love about you. Your big heart."

I rolled my eyes. "Terrence …" I was about to end the call, but he kept talking.

"By the way, would you mind if I came by for a little while?"

Hell yeah, I mind. "Umm, I don't think that's a good idea."

"I really just want to talk. Some things have happened since we spoke last month, and I wanted to catch you up."

"You can say whatever it is you have to say on this phone, right now."

"Please, Anisa," he begged. "I promise I won't try anything. I just need to see you face-to-face."

Dammit! Dammit! Dammit! Tell him you don't give a damn. Tell him you've moved on. Say something!

"Okay," was all I could utter.

"Okay, give me about an hour and I'll be right over."

CHAPTER 19

How's Your Eye?

I wanted to make sure I was cute, but I wasn't going to overdo it and have him think I was getting all dolled up for him. I put on one of my long sundresses, fixed my hair, and put some foundation and lip gloss on my face and looked in the mirror. *Yeah, that's good enough.* That's all the work I was going to put into my appearance this evening because he didn't deserve my efforts anymore. I'd decided to give him only five minutes to say everything he had to say, and then he had to go. If he tried to stay longer, my excuse would be that I had to go to work the next morning and I needed to look over my files before I went in the next day.

When I opened the door, he didn't disappoint. As usual, Terrence was looking so good, I wanted to take a bite. I felt the butterflies all over again but refused to let him see me sweat. I was cool as a fan. Well, I hoped I was playing it cool.

I opened the door wider and stepped aside for him to enter. I took a deep breath as he breezed past me, smelling as good as he looked. *Slick dog,* I thought. He was wearing the Dior Sauvage I had gifted him for Christmas. He knew I loved that shit. I could tell he didn't know if he should hug me, and I stood my ground because I didn't think he should. If my body was reacting to just seeing him, I couldn't imagine what him touching me would do to me.

He spoke first. "Anisa, it's so good seeing you. You look amazing."

"Thanks, Terrence. You're looking pretty good yourself."

"I've really missed you."

I didn't reply. He strolled over to the dining table, put his hands on one of the chair backs, and looked back at me. "May I?"

I nodded, and he pulled it out as I stood there watching. He motioned to the chair. "Can you please sit?"

I slowly made my way over and sat down. Damn. I should've had a drink.

He pulled out the chair beside me and sat down as well.

I intertwined my fingers and rested them on the dining table as I waited for him to speak. He reached over and put his hand on mine. I wanted to pull away but decided to let him speak first. *This had better be good.*

"Letting you go was a huge mistake."

You damned right! "Mm-hmm," I answered, but I was unmoved. He had to do a hell of a lot better than that.

"I'm sorry that I said what I said about no man wanting you. It was cruel and I spoke out of anger."

"Yes, it was cruel," I agreed.

He hung his head. "It was, and I kick myself every day for that."

I wanted to kick you, too, but I think I did a good job with your eye. "Okay."

He paused as he contemplated his next words. "I want you back."

"Terrence."

"Before you say anything, I want you to know that Asha and I are no more."

Mm-hmm, so she no longer wants your ass. "Oh, really? So what happened?"

"She got tired of me talking about you, and we finally agreed that we aren't good for each other and should just co-parent Mikel."

"Mm-hmm."

"I know I'd have to prove myself, but I also know there are great things ahead of us, Anisa, and if you give me a chance, I'd like to show you."

"Like what, Terrence?"

"Like marriage and kids."

I was speechless, but I wasn't going to let him suck me in that easily. In all actuality, if Zahair wasn't in the picture, I might've jumped at the chance of marrying Terrence because that's what I'd wanted all along. But the truth was that Zahair was in the picture, and I was feeling things for him I wasn't ready to give up on yet.

I finally removed my hands from Terrence's touch. What if he changed his mind and decided to go back to Asha, or worse, got bored with me and found another woman? I didn't want to feel that pain again. "I need some time."

He nodded. "The fact that you even took the time to see me is well appreciated, and I'll never give up on us." He stood up slowly, and I was glad he didn't push, because I had never felt so perplexed in my almost-thirty years.

I stood up as well and walked him to the door. He opened it and stepped outside and before I knew it, he leaned over and brushed a light kiss on my lips. I froze, and before I could say anything, he said, "I'll call you soon." With that, he walked away.

That night, I tossed and turned as I thought about my situation. Here it was: I had two men that I could possibly make a future with. Terrence was stable, and we had almost three years behind us. I felt he cared about me, but I wasn't sure he genuinely loved me. Furthermore, he was a cheater and cheaters didn't change their stripes overnight.

Then there was Zahair. He was damn-near everything I could hope for; he treated me like a queen and made me feel like one as well, but I felt he might be a little overbearing. Besides that, our relationship history was mostly in college, and we were both grown now and didn't live in the same city, nor were either of us willing to relocate any time soon, so that might put us at an impasse.

Years ago, I would've killed to have options like this, but it wasn't so fun now that I was actually in this situation.

CHAPTER 20

Bring That Ole Thing Back

After a hectic day at work the next day, I called Zahair.

"Hey, you," I said.

"Hey, yourself," he answered, but his tone wasn't convincing, and I couldn't tell if he was happy to hear from me or not.

"I miss you already," I said.

He sighed, and his tone softened. "I miss you, too, Anisa."

We spoke for a while, but when I opened my mouth to talk about how stressful my job had been that day, he cut me off.

"Umm, Anisa. I need to take this call. I'll call you back."

Wow, okay.

He never called me back that night and after his abrupt exit, I wasn't sure if it was just my mind or what, but I could tell something was off.

After an even more hectic day at work the day after, Iya called. I was glad to hear from her because I was so busy that I hadn't spoken to her in a few days—not to mention I had something to run by her. She was actually the perfect person to give me some insight, because I figured she may have been in this situation a time or two in her life, and I wouldn't dare tell anyone else that I was even entertaining the possibility of giving Terrence another chance.

"Hey, sunshine!" she sang.

"Hey, Iya," I sang back.

"I just wanted to check on you because I haven't heard from you in a few days."

"I know. I'm sorry, but work has been crazy."

"No apologies necessary, queen. I know how life can be at times."

"Thanks."

"Sure." She continued, "On a more exciting note, I can't wait for your birthday party on Saturday. I have something special planned at Lorna's."

I knew she was going to blow me away with one of her performances and I welcomed it. I also looked forward to seeing everyone. Nia said she would be in town, and I was happy Jamie was coming in as well.

I decided to ask my question without mentioning any names. "Iya, may I ask you something?"

"Of course, queen. You can ask me anything."

I took a deep breath and spoke before I changed my mind. "Have you ever been in love with more than one man?"

I knew the answer, but I preferred to let her tell me her version.

She was silent for a moment, but she answered, "My child, whew! Too many times to count."

"And how did you deal with that? Did you do the good ole pros and cons list?"

"I've done that, too, but it didn't quite give me the answers I needed."

Wow! The next step is a therapist for me. I asked, "So, what did you do?"

Again, the line went silent and when she came back, she simply answered, "I chose myself."

I loved my iya to death, but as usual she was being too deep for me and speaking in parables, so I asked, "How did you choose yourself?"

"I chose to do what would make me happy."

I pondered her statement. "Weren't you afraid of ending up alone?"

"Young queen, sometimes choosing yourself can be one of the hardest choices of your life, so yes."

Sounds like a lonely, selfish place, I thought. "I don't want to end up alone, Iya."

The line went quiet for a moment again, and when she came back, she kept dropping nuggets.

"When you get to a place where you are whole, you'll never be lonely because you'll have everything inside of you to be your own best company." She went on, "And a person who is whole is rarely alone for too long because knowing and loving yourself is a beauty that's infectious. That's when you usually meet the person or persons you desire."

What she was saying was a bit too much for me that night, especially after being drained from work. "Okay," I answered.

"Why did you ask me about being in love with more than one man?"

I gave her a brief overview of the conversation I'd had with Zahair about relocating and how he urged me to pursue a singing career. Then I told her about speaking with Terrence.

She listened intently and when I was done, she replied, "Okay. May I add one more thing?"

"Sure."

"I've never told you this, but out of all my children, you're the one most like me."

I was surprised to hear that because I was so structured and tried to plan every detail of my life down to the tee.

"Why do you say that?"

She sighed. "Well, I wasn't always this confident because I got made fun of for my dark skin as a child."

I raised my eyebrows and sat with my mouth wide open because there was no one who was more confident that my iya.

Before I could interject, she continued, "I also thought I had all the answers and tried to play by *the rules* as well, but I quickly learned that rules were meant to be broken."

I hoped she wasn't talking about my love life, because I wasn't even trying to hear about being with more than one man.

"And I wasn't talking about your love life, I just meant life in general."

I laughed. Iya knew me so well.

I breathed a sigh of relief.

I was still baffled that she had ever lacked in confidence. After several moments of silence, I asked, "Iya, why didn't you ever tell me that you got made fun of as a child?"

She puffed out air then answered, "I'm not sure. I just figured that if I got you to focus on something you're meant to do, you wouldn't be so hard on yourself."

My mind was blown. "Well, how did you manage to become so confident?" I asked.

"Hmm. Well, you know how the saying goes: sometimes you have to fake it until you make it. Furthermore, I realized early on that I was put on this earth to inspire others through song, so I knew that since God gave me this voice, I was also made exactly how I should be. Beautiful, and perfectly imperfect."

"Wow," was all I could say.

"Yes, queen. God don't make no junk," she added lightheartedly. She didn't miss a beat when she added, "But anyways, in regards to Zahair, no man is perfect, and I don't want to tell you what you should do. But Zahair definitely has a point and might be just what you need."

"Which point are you talking about?"

"When he said you need to live out your passion."

I rolled my eyes. *Here we go.* She was going to start pushing singing on me again.

"You were meant to sing, and I know this from the look in your eyes every time you get on stage."

"It's fear you see in my eyes, Iya."

"Hmm. I don't know. It may start out that way, but tell me this. Once you open your mouth and get going, do you still feel afraid?"

I pondered her question, and she was right. The initial fear I felt always dissipated after the first few notes.

"I guess I don't."

Before I had time to think about it, she asked, "I don't want to put any pressure on you, but do you think you'd be open to doing a song or two with your old girl on Saturday?"

I thought about it. It was my birthday, my thirtieth no less. *What the hell,* I thought. I threw caution to the wind. I was entering a new decade of my life and this was supposed to be my time to be fearless. "Sure, Iya," I replied.

"Really?" she asked in disbelief. I had surprised her, and I was happy that her seeing me on stage again could bring her so much joy.

She spoke hurriedly, probably because she thought I would change my mind. "Okay, I'll send the tracks over shortly!"

After our call, I lay awake, staring at the ceiling for a while at the revelation that anyone could ever make fun of Iya's beautiful skin. She was damn-near perfect in my eyes. Before I dozed off, the last thing I remember thinking was, *If they could make fun of her, I don't have a chance.*

CHAPTER 21

I'm on my Own

My workload continued to grow, and it was getting harder to devote time to speaking to Zahair. Plus, after our last conversation ended so abruptly, I didn't know how to approach him. I was surprised that I hadn't heard from him in several days, which wasn't like him. With each conversation, I could sense he was getting impatient, and I couldn't say that I blamed him, considering that we started off speaking almost every day after I returned from DC.

I also noticed that if I didn't call, he didn't take the initiative to call either. When I worked up the nerve to ask him what happened several nights before, and why he didn't call me back, he simply said, "I fell asleep." There was no remorse in his tone, and I felt that I was losing him. After a few lackluster conversations with him, I was still unclear about where we were headed. It didn't take long before he made the decision for both of us. After speaking with him this particular evening, I remarked, "These people are sucking me dry. I barely have time for myself."

"Mm-hmm."

"Mm-hmm? Zahair, I basically just told you that these people are trying to work me to death, and all you can say is mm-hmm?"

"Anisa, I don't know what more you want me to say."

"Oh, I don't know. Say you understand. Say you support me and feel my pain. Say that you feel sorry for me, but dammit, say something besides mm-hmm!"

He sighed. "I can't say something that I don't feel, because we all have choices. I'm a builder, Anisa, and I won't make excuses for you continuing to be unhappy."

The fact that he cared so much was one of the things I loved about him, but it was also one of the things that was making me hate him at that moment. He was truly pissing me off.

"Oh, so if I'm not doing what *you* want, or what *you* think should make me happy, then you don't want to hear what I have to say?"

"That's not fair," he replied.

"Umph," I muttered.

There was an awkward silence, and I realized our fantastic voyage was about to come to an end.

"Anisa," he sighed.

"Yes, Zahair."

"Before you left DC, you agreed that you wanted to see where this could go. Right?"

"I did."

"Well, since you went back home, all you do is complain about work, but I haven't seen you make any effort in changing your current situation. I don't know where I fit into your life."

Now I was on the defensive. "Now that's not fair, Zahair. I have to earn a living."

"And this is true, but you can do that and be happy at the same time if that's what you choose."

I rolled my eyes. *Here we go again.*

"Zahair, you just don't understand."

"Then make me understand," he prodded.

The line grew silent. We were both frustrated, but he completely messed me up when he said, "Look, Anisa, maybe we should give each other some space."

Wow! I was surprised he would take it there. I opened my mouth to object but changed my mind. Instead, I answered, "Yes, maybe we should do that."

My feelings were hurt, and in that moment, I made up all kinds of excuses. Maybe he and I were just too different to be together, I told myself. After an hour, though, I changed my mind. When I really thought about it, I realized no one had ever treated me the way he did or made me feel the way he did every time we were together. I dialed his number, but it went straight to voicemail. I called twice more, and it did the same thing, and it didn't take long for me to realize he'd blocked me.

Asshole! I thought, and I let a tear fall from my eye when I realized I had probably just missed out on my blessing.

Saturday arrived, and I woke up from a slight hangover from downing several glasses of wine with Jamie the night before. My phone rang at 8:30 a.m. I silenced it, but it kept ringing and the texts kept coming in, and I realized it was my birthday. I rubbed my eyes, yawned, and sat up.

"Thank you, God, for giving me thirty years on this earth."

My phone rang again. It was Monique. "I know you're not still sleeping, bestie. It's your birthday, biatch!"

I laughed. "Thanks, Mo."

"Yeah, we about to get all the way turnt up tonight!" she said excitedly.

"I know. Yay," I answered dryly.

"I look forward to meeting you and Jamie for brunch," she replied.

"Okay, hon," I said.

The line beeped. "Mo, let me get this call. See you soon."

"Okay. Later!"

When I clicked over, Nia, Talia, and Iya were all on the line. They shouted, "Happy birthday!" in unison.

Mom: "Happy Earth, strong young queen!"

Nia: "Happy birthday, sis!"

Talia: "Happy thirtieth birthday, big head!"

Me: "Thanks, ladies."

My phone buzzed.

"It's Daddy. Hold on." I connected him.

"Hey, Dad, I'm on the line with Nia, Talia, and Iya."

"Well, hey, my girls," he answered. "Oh, and you too, Amina."

We all laughed.

He exclaimed, "Happy birthday to my angel!"

"Thanks, Daddy! I can't wait to see everyone tonight."

"Yes, I can't wait to see you beautiful young ladies tonight as well." He added again, "Oh, and you too, Amina."

Again, we cracked up laughing.

The five of us spoke for a while, and I hung up to go and see what Jamie was doing. I could hear her laughing through my guest room door. When I knocked, I heard her tell whoever was on the line that she'd call them back.

She came to the door cheesing, with her wild hair all around her face. "Happy birthday, bestie!" she yelled and hugged me.

"Thanks, friend." I hugged her back.

She was usually a late sleeper, so I was surprised she was already up—on a phone call, no less, but I knew why. I smiled because she was glowing.

"Tyrone?" I asked.

She cheesed and answered excitedly, "Yes, girl!"

I smiled back and nodded. She didn't talk about it often with me because Zahair and I were no longer in correspondence, and she didn't want to rub it in my face, but I was genuinely happy that things were going so well for her and Tyrone. She had mentioned on a few occasions how things were going so well, in fact, that they were thinking of taking their relationship to the next level in the next few months with either him moving to New York, or her moving back to DC. I had never seen my friend so content, and it amazed me that she was even thinking about moving, especially considering how independent she was.

As I was getting ready to go to brunch, Terrence called.

"Happy thirtieth birthday, beautiful!" he exclaimed.

He'd done a good job of giving me my space and falling back, and I appreciated that, but I was glad to hear from him.

"Thanks, Terrence."

"Of course. I couldn't let your very special day pass and not speak to you. What do you have planned today?"

I informed him of my brunch plans, and that later, I would be going by Lorna's to hear my mother perform.

He answered, "That sounds awesome! Maybe I'll see you later then."

He wasn't asking, but we hadn't made plans to do anything, so I didn't give what he was saying much thought. I wasn't about to ask him either. "Okay, sure."

We hung up, and Jamie and I headed out to meet up with Monique at one of my favorite restaurants, Just Spoons Café in Plantation. After feasting on my Honey Butta Fried Chicken Sandwich and a mimosa, I sat around with the girls, making small talk. Monique gifted me with some custom-made lip gloss, lipstick, and foundation from one of my favorite cosmetic lines.

Then she let us know that she was thinking of taking some courses in billing and coding so she could have more options bringing money in. We were happy to hear she was trying to do something else because it didn't seem like she wanted to be at her job much longer. She also let us know she had found a new guy she was really feeling.

"He just gets me, you know?" she added.

I was truly excited for her. I had to meet and shake that brother's hand, because any man strong enough to handle Monique must have Superman powers.

"So, what about you, Anisa?" they inquired. "Have you spoken to Zahair?"

I let them know I hadn't tried his number again after I realized he'd blocked me, but I missed him terribly.

"I can ask Tyrone to reach out to him, if you'd like?" Jamie offered, but I wasn't trying to hear it. He had many chances to reach out if he really wanted to, and I hadn't received any calls or texts from him. Believe me, I'd been checking. I wasn't going into thirty being desperate; besides, my mind was leaning on giving Terrence one more chance anyway. I would never tell them that, though.

CHAPTER 22

On Bended Knee

The night of my party arrived, and I was excited to wear the dress Jamie had gifted me for my party. Monique had to run a few errands after we finished eating, so Jamie had taken me to the mall afterwards and had me try on a few dresses. Her model expertise was right on point because when I tried on this black number, I was impressed with my reflection. As I stood on my tippy toes and modeled in the mirror, I realized that although I wasn't the size I wanted to be, I was a beautiful woman. I'd cut my hair short after I came back from DC, and I had to admit this short hair looked awesome on me. It accentuated my high cheekbones, and I also loved how convenient it was to just wake up and rub a little Curl Smoothie in it and go. This way, I got to see my natural curls as well. I yelled, "Jamie, come look!"

I opened the door to the fitting room and her face lit up. "Oh my goodness, Anisa!" she exclaimed. "You look absolutely gorgeous! You can't leave that dress!"

And I felt it, too.

That night, she hooked my makeup up, and we were out. When we arrived, I was delighted to see how many of my friends and family had come out to support me and, of course, hear my mother do her thing. Iya had hired a local event planning company, and they had the place immaculately decked out. I didn't know she was going to do all of that, but I should've known she wouldn't have done anything less for me. Iya put her heart into everything she touched.

My hands shook and I began to sweat as I went over the tracks in my head that my mother had sent over as I waited for her to call me on stage.

Iya was singing with Miami's own Live Poet's Society tonight, and they were amazing. The band dedicated several songs to me, and the poets recited several poems to me as well. I was touched. Closer to the end of the show, I grew more anxious because I knew Iya would call me up at any moment. When she finished and invited me on stage, I felt as though I would throw up, but I wiped my clammy palms on my dress and made my way to the front as I cursed myself for allowing Iya to talk me into this.

The music started and Iya sang the first few lines of the song, then she gave the signal for me to come in. I took a deep breath and could feel my voice trembling when I began, but I found my center and a miracle happened. After the first few seconds, I closed my eyes and felt as if my feet were no longer touching the ground. It was orgasmic as I felt the melody flowing through my body and I sang louder. I opened my eyes and looked out at the crowd, but I was not afraid. I watched as the audience closed their eyes and swayed to the music as the notes effortlessly flowed from my mouth. So, this is what they meant by the euphoric feeling you get when you're doing something you love. Now I got it. I had finally experienced the breakthrough I had spent my whole life searching for.

I was so engrossed in the music that I hadn't seen Terrence come in. He had a beautiful bouquet in his hands, and he closed his eyes and swayed to the music along with everyone else.

When I finished the song, the crowd stood and applauded loudly. I blushed and felt gratitude to my creator for giving me this gift. I hugged my mother tightly as she wiped away her tears and whispered, "Anisa, that was absolutely amazing!"

I wiped my eyes and said, "Thank you, Iya. For everything."

As I began to step away from our performance area, Terrence made his way to the front and grabbed my hand. I looked up just in time to see the look on Monique's face as she crossed her arms and twisted her neck. I also caught a glimpse of Talia's and my father's faces as well. None of them looked pleased. Terrence held on to my hand as I plastered a smile on my face and said through gritted teeth, "What're you doing here?"

He handed me the bouquet. "You'll see." He ran over and grabbed the mic. "I just wanted to take the time to wish this beautiful woman right here a happy thirtieth birthday!" he gushed. "She's been awesome to me, and I wanted to let you all know how much I appreciate her."

Oh damn. This isn't good.

"And one more thing," he added as he walked over to me. He got down on one knee and I almost fainted because I realized what he was about to do. I thought I heard a record scratch as he looked up at me and asked, "Anisa, will you marry me?"

I hadn't seen him with a drink, so I figured he was sober, but still, I searched his face to see if he was serious. I glanced around as I waited for Ashton Kutcher to jump out and tell me I was being punk'd.

I had waited for Terrence to say those words to me for three long years now, but I never thought it would happen like this. I was also too caught up in the moment to think about the repercussions of accepting his impromptu marriage proposal. Tears formed in my eyes as I cried, "Yes, Terrence! I'll marry you!" He stood up and kissed me.

My father stormed toward us, and Adebayo and Darius ran over to restrain him. Talia damn-near fainted and Nia caught her. Jamie stood there with a puzzled expression on her face, and I heard Monique cursing from the other side of the room. Iya's face was the last one I saw. She shook her head in disappointment. Terrence had just turned our beautiful moment into a shit show.

The audience thought it was exciting because they didn't know our history, and they cheered at his performance, but none of my close friends and family were pleased. After holding my hand and going around the restaurant thanking several of the patrons, Terrence must have sensed the tension in the air because he kissed me and let me know he would call me later. He left soon thereafter. I imagine he felt uncomfortable knowing there were several people in the building who wanted to hurt him.

When my daddy gained his composure, he walked over to me after Terrence made his exit, and I could tell how disappointed he was by the way he looked at me. I was thankful he didn't say it at that time, though, because I just wanted to try and enjoy the moment. He hugged me and told me he loved me but let me know we would definitely be discussing this matter at a later date.

Talia was completely pissed and didn't have a problem letting me know. "How could you agree to marry that loser after all he's done to you?" she fumed.

"He wouldn't have asked me to marry him if he wasn't ready," I tried to assure her, but I had to admit, I wasn't too sure of that myself.

"This time, I won't be there to pick up the pieces when he drops you on your ass!" she spat.

Darius tried to make me feel better. "Congratulations!" he said and smiled uneasily at me. Talia shot him a death stare, but he said, "Come on, baby," and tried to not to make eye contact with her as he ushered her out of the restaurant.

I was hurt, but I got it.

Nia hugged me awkwardly. "Well, you're finally getting what you wanted." Then she added, "I sure hope he's worth it."

I wasn't sure how I should feel about her comment.

The last person I spoke to before I left Lorna's was Iya.

"Are you going to fuss at me, too?" I asked.

She looked tired. "No, queen. You're an intelligent and beautiful woman who can make choices for herself. God knows I've made a few mistakes in my time."

Mistakes? Terrence wasn't a mistake. He was a man who loved and wanted to marry me.

"Thanks for your support, Iya," I said, and we embraced. "This night has been one of the most enlightening ones of my life. I'm so happy, and I just wish everyone else could be happy for me."

She gave me a half smile. "I know your father and Talia weren't pleased, but they'll come around."

"I don't know about that."

"Well, they'll have to deal with it if this is what you choose."

I loved my iya. She always knew what to say to make me feel better. I hugged her again and left with Jamie and Monique to finish out my birthday night.

Monique was pissed, but because she was a ride-or-die kind of friend, she didn't change her mind about us hanging out, although I could tell from her demeanor that I'd be hearing about it for the rest of the night. She fussed from the back seat the whole way as we drove to Miami Beach to finish off my birthday celebration. "You can't be serious, Anisa!"

"Can I just enjoy this moment without all of your harassment?" I asked.

"Hell nah!" she spat.

I was excited to be engaged, but I wasn't sure if I was fond of how Terrence had chosen to do it, especially being that we hadn't discussed it much since our breakup. Not to mention, he hadn't spoken to my father and asked him for my hand like they did in the old school days. We all knew what the answer would've been if he did, though. How does a strong *hell no* sound?

I was so caught up in the moment, and excited about his proposal, that I hadn't taken all of those things into consideration at the time, but I was officially an engaged woman. Tonight, all my dreams were finally coming true.

I stared at my beautiful ring and felt mixed emotions. He'd done well in getting the ring we'd talked about on numerous occasions, and I hoped his proposal in front of everyone meant he was finally ready to be with just me. I mean, he wouldn't have done that if he wasn't ready, right? I told myself that over and over.

Jamie was quiet for the most part as she drove, and she finally spoke only to ask, "Anisa, are you sure this is what you want? I mean, you two have only spoken once since your breakup."

"Well—"

Monique didn't wait for me to finish. "Oh, hell nah!" she

fussed and threw up her hands. "So, you've been talking to his ass all this time, and didn't tell us? Now I see I was right about the real reason you didn't want to move to DC."

"I spoke to him only a few times other than the time I mentioned, but I've only seen Terrence once since I've been back," I muttered, and I regretted it as soon as it came out my mouth.

"You saw him, too? Really, Anisa!" Monique exclaimed even louder this time. "How could you keep that from us? Where, when?"

I glanced back at her. "Does it matter?" I asked.

She rolled her eyes. "Whatever, Anisa ..."

We rode with only the sound of the radio playing for a few moments, but she wouldn't let it die. "Well, what about Zahair? Don't you still care about him?"

There it was. His handsome face appeared in my mind for the hundredth time since I'd spoken to him last. The man who had shown me how it felt to be truly appreciated and adored. The man who wanted more for me than I wanted for myself—the man whom I loved.

"Of course I do, but Zahair gave up on us, so he showed me what he was really about," I said. I figured that if I said it enough, I would believe it, and I tried to convince myself I was ready to move on with Terrence. But my soul yearned for Zahair, and I missed him more than I was willing to admit to myself or anyone else.

CHAPTER 23

The Intervention

After enjoying the rest of a somewhat-tense night, I woke up good and hungover around noon the next day. "Was this all a dream?" I asked myself, but the diamond on my left ring finger let me know that it wasn't.

I had several voice messages.

The first one was from Terrence. "I know you're probably knocked out, but I'm excited to talk to my wife-to-be. Call me when you get up."

"Wife-to-be, fiancé, I'm going to be Mrs. Anisa Atkins," I repeated over and over. I couldn't believe I was really going to be someone's wife.

The next message was from my iya. "Hey, queen, I just

wanted to make sure you made it in safely. Last night was wonderful—well, for the most part, that is. Talk later."

The next was from my father. He said, "Call me when you can. I want to see if you'll be available later today because we need to talk."

So much for my birthday bliss. I was pretty sure I knew what he wanted to talk about. I called my daddy back immediately because I didn't want him to come looking for me.

"Hey, birthday princess," he answered.

I smiled. "Good afternoon, Daddy."

"Did you enjoy the rest of your night?"

"Yes."

"Good. So, I want to come by later. Will you be available around six?"

Here it goes. Man, he didn't waste any time. "Okay. What do you want to talk about?"

"Last night."

Dammit. "Okay. I'll be here."

"Okay, love. I'll see you then."

"Okay, Daddy."

I got up and went to the restroom to freshen up and find something to help me feel better because I was feeling a little nauseous. When I came out, Jamie was already in the kitchen.

She laughed. "Hey, girl. Welcome back to the land of the living."

"Oh my goodness. Yes, last night was definitely something else! My stomach is messed all the way up. I see Mo's still out."

Monique was sprawled out on my couch. She had stayed over because she was too drunk to drive home. I mean, my girl was really tossing the drinks back last night. You would've thought it was *her* birthday by the way she was acting, and I felt partially responsible. She was drinking like that because of me and how disappointed she was about Terrence's proposal.

"Yeah, well, I'm about to make you ladies my favorite hangover cure." Jamie had carrots and apples on the counter. "Do you have any ginger around here?"

Again, I was thankful for my mother and her healthy habits for always looking out. She had just given me some the other day. I took the ginger out of the fridge and handed it to Jamie. "What are you making?" I asked.

"I'm just going to blend these carrots, apple, and the ginger together. It'll help settle your stomach, trust me."

I scrunched my face up.

"What?" she asked, laughing.

"Doesn't sound too appetizing."

"You know, Anisa, I'm not trying to preach, but you need to take better care of yourself. You know I'm all about healthy eating. In fact, I wanted to ask you if we could ride by that vegan spot in North Miami Beach you took me to the last time. Hakim something, is it?"

I chuckled. "You mean Vegetarian Restaurant by Hakin."

"Yeah, that."

Mo finally began to show signs of life. "Ohhh, my head," she moaned.

"I'm about to get you fixed up right now," Jamie said as she turned on the blender.

"It's too loud! Oh my goodness! It's too loud!" Monique slurred as she held her head.

Jamie and I giggled, and I decided to use that moment to call Terrence. "Be right back," I announced.

I went in my room and closed the door and called him.

"Hey, wife-to-be," he answered.

I blushed. Those words sounded so good. "Hey, you."

"So how did you enjoy the rest of your night?" he asked.

"It was good. Awkward, but good. Terrence, although I'm excited to be your wife, I wish we would've discussed this before you proposed in front of my family and friends."

"I know," he said, "but what better time to propose than on your birthday? Your thirtieth birthday, no less."

He was a cocky one. What made him think I would say yes after all he'd put me through? "Well, we need to talk about what we're going to do going forward."

"Yes, ma'am," he teased.

"Anyway, I'm going to have to call you back. I have to go remedy my hangover and hang out with my girls for a bit before my father comes by."

He chuckled. "Damn, that bad, huh?"

"Yeah. That bad."

We made definitive plans to talk later that evening because we still had a multitude of things to discuss, and I went to the kitchen to drink my dreaded mix from Jamie.

By the time 5:30 rolled around, I was trying to decide if I needed army fatigues because I knew it was about to be a fight when my father came. What I didn't know was that he wasn't coming alone. He knocked on the door and when I looked through the peephole, I saw my iya, Talia, and Nia as well.

What in the hell? I had been set up. I took a deep breath and opened the door.

"Hey, angel." My father's stern face greeted me. He hugged me and kissed my forehead.

"Hey, Daddy."

My mother was behind him. She smiled and hugged me. "Hey, young queen."

"Hey, Mommy."

Nia hugged me and greeted me as well.

Last, but not least, was Talia. She and her belly breezed past me with no words and her face screwed up.

I said, "Hey, Lia."

"Umph," was her response.

I looked awkwardly at them as they stood around, waiting. I tried to laugh it off. "If I knew you all were coming, I would've cleaned up a bit."

No one cracked a smile.

Jamie was seated at the table, and Monique propped herself up on the couch and sipped tea from one of my coffee cups. I hadn't asked them to leave because I figured this wouldn't take long, but when I realized otherwise, I looked back at them. "Do you mind giving us a minute? I think my family wants to talk to me in private."

"Oh no, I told Monique and Jamie to stay. They're family, too," Talia said.

I took a few deep breaths so I wouldn't get upset. "I guess all of you should find yourselves seats."

I looked back at Jamie, and she mouthed the words, "I'm sorry," and Monique propped herself up and said nothing, but she looked pretty smug. I swallowed what it was I really wanted to say when I realized everyone knew about this except for me.

After everyone got seated, they went in on me.

Daddy: "I want to know what's really going on with this man."

Nia: "Are you sure Terrence is what you want? I mean, look at my life."

Talia: "What were you thinking?"

Iya: "Are you sure this is really what you want, and who you want it with?"

I felt ambushed.

Me: "We've been talking, and we realized that we want to be together." Well, it was partially true. We did talk, but *he* did most of the talking, and *he* made the decision for both of us the night before.

Monique: "What about his baby mama?"

Talia: "Yeah, that."

Nia sat there watching as we went back and forth, and her smug expression showed she was just taking this all in. She seemed to be loving every minute of it.

Me: "He let me know they're no longer together."

Talia: "And you believed him?"

Monique: "So, he wants you now, being that she no longer wants his ass."

I had to admit I thought the same thing at first. I never wanted to be anyone's second choice, but I convinced myself he wouldn't propose unless he was ready to move on with me. Hell, she may have the baby, but I had the ring.

Me: "No. He wants me because he loves me and sees that I'm the better woman for him."

There was a collective sigh in the room.

Talia shook her head and covered her face with her hand. "Oh my God, how ignorant can you really be?"

Iya: "Talia, that's not helping."

Daddy: "All I know is that if this Terrence guy hurts you again, I can't be held responsible for my actions."

Iya: "Khalil, you know that's not the answer."

Daddy: "It's my answer."

They were doing too much, and I was getting angry. I couldn't believe no one was supporting me. People made mistakes and none of us was perfect in this room. Iya and Nia should definitely know that. After all, they'd done their share of cheating in their lifetime. I was thirty now, and I didn't need anyone trying to dictate my life for me anymore.

I was so overwhelmed with being ganged up on that before I knew it, I blurted out, "Iya hasn't been perfect in her relationships, and while everyone is going in on my relationship with Terrence, how come no one has mentioned that Nia is having an affair?"

For the second day in a row, I heard a non-existent record scratch as everyone's mouths dropped, and I regretted those words as soon as they left my mouth.

Talia scowled at me. "Damn, Anisa. I can't believe you! I told you that in confidence!"

"Oh my goodness. I'm so sorry, Lia," I began as I started to walk over to her.

She put her hand up. "I'm good!" she fumed. She got up, grabbed her purse, and made her way to the door. "I'm done with this!" She yelled over her shoulder. "I'll be in the car when y'all are ready because I'm tired of trying to save somebody that doesn't want to be saved." With that, she walked out and slammed the door behind her.

All eyes were now on me, and Nia was looking pissed off as well. She had tears in her eyes when she added sarcastically, "Well, since everyone knows about my affair, I might as well let you all know that my man's name is Devon, and I had a miscarriage as well." She got up and stormed out behind Talia.

Miscarriage? No way. Nia had a miscarriage? I didn't even know she'd been pregnant. Why hadn't anyone shared that information with me? I felt completely dissed and dismissed.

I stood in shocked silence at her announcement.

Monique and Jamie stared at each other with raised eyebrows and open mouths. Monique looked down into her cup and said, "Well damn, I'm not thirsty anymore. I just got all the tea I needed."

My daddy closed his eyes, leaned forward, clasped his hands together, and rested his chin on his hands. He didn't speak for a few tense moments, and I was afraid of what he would say when he did. When he opened his eyes, disappointment was written all over his face.

He stood up slowly, took a deep breath, and gave his last pitch. "For the most part, you've been a daughter that's always made good decisions for her life, but for some reason, you keep dropping the ball on your love life. For the life of me, I can't understand it."

"Daddy—"

"Let me finish. I'm going to say this, and then I'm done. Before you go down the aisle with this man, I suggest you take some time out and make sure you know without a shadow of a doubt that it's you he really wants, because we men don't change overnight."

Ouch.

He gave me a quick kiss on my forehead and made his way out the door.

I stared at my iya, and she stared back at me with sad eyes. She was always my cheerleader even when everyone else turned their back on me, but I had a feeling today was going to be different.

Her nose flared as she spoke, which was rare for my usually calm iya. She stated, "I'm disappointed in you. I knew about your sister's infidelity, but that wasn't your business to tell. Everyone here took the time out today because we all love you and want the best for you. I can understand you feeling the way you feel about what I've done to our family, but I wish you wouldn't have put your sister's business out on front street. She's dealing with enough from her miscarriage, and this was not the time for that. Plus, this moment is about you."

As she scolded me, I hung my head and tears welled up

in my eyes. I felt myself growing smaller. All of the arrogance I previously had dissipated with every piercing word.

My tears didn't deter her. She used her hands to emphasize her words as she continued, "You need to take a good look at the discord you're allowing this man to cause in your life, even without him being present today. I was hoping to gain a son, but it feels like I'm losing a daughter. I hope you figure out what demons are causing you to make these poor decisions before you do something you'll live to regret and lose everyone that means something to you." She hugged me tight for several agonizing moments then she made her way out the door behind everyone else.

I rolled my eyes at Jamie and Monique because I didn't appreciate them not telling me that my family was planning an intervention, but I got it. They did it because they cared about me. After everyone left, Monique hugged me and left shortly after, and Jamie and I left so I could take her to the airport. We rode in silence, and I only spoke to ask, "Why do you think they'd keep something like her being pregnant a secret? Nia and I aren't that close, but damn."

Jamie shrugged and looked over at me. "I don't know. Maybe they were trying to spare you."

"Spare me? From what?"

She shrugged again. "Maybe from feeling that everyone else was having the one thing you've wanted for so long. You two have always had a strained relationship. Maybe they didn't want you to feel that she had one up on you again."

Damn. I felt like the worst person in the world.

CHAPTER 24

Where do Broken Hearts Go?

When I got back home that night, I felt confused and lonely. I called Terrence and he came right over. Over the next two weeks, things were good between the two of us. He listened as I vented about how my family felt about everything, and he said he hoped he didn't get me in trouble with my family because he knew some of them weren't fond of him. Not once did he offer to go with me and speak with them, though. In my opinion, that's what a real man would've done.

Sexually, though, he helped me feel better—minus orally, of course. He promised that would change once we got married. I highly doubted that, and honestly, every time he touched me, all I could think about was how Zahair had made me feel when we were together. I knew there was nothing Terrence could do at this point that could make me truly forget about Zahair.

We spent most of the time going between our homes, and I gave him a copy of my key even though I was still waiting for him to do the same for his home. He stayed with me some nights and I stayed with him, and we even began making wedding plans. I realized things were still off in some areas when I asked him when he was going to finally bring his son around.

He seemed uncomfortable with that and simply told me "soon enough." I really began to feel a way, though, when one weekend he told me he would have Mikel.

"Oh great. Well, why don't I come over and cook something and spend a little time with the two of you?" I suggested.

"I don't know if I'm ready to bring anyone around my son yet." He was adamant.

I was dumbfounded. "I'm not just anyone, Terrence. I'm your fiancé. And how do you suppose I bond with him if I'm never around him?"

"I know, baby, I'm going to figure it out, and it'll be soon. I promise."

I was annoyed, but I decided to drop it for that day. "Okay, just know that we can't get married if I don't know your son."

"Of course, my love," he assured me.

I had reached out to Talia a time or two, but she still wasn't speaking to me. I knew it was a combination of me taking Terrence back, telling everyone something she told me in confidence, and the pregnancy hormones, because we had never not spoken for this long and I missed her.

I had also reached out to Nia and although she answered my call, I could tell she was still not happy with me. I apologized for taking my anger out on her that day and let her know I was even sorrier for what she was going through with the miscarriage. I couldn't imagine her pain because, like me, she was also yearning to be a mother. She told me she appreciated my apology, and she also admitted she had gotten pregnant from her new man, Devon. She said that at another time, she would tell me more. It was a lot to take in, but I understood she didn't owe me an explanation, so I didn't pry.

My parents were still consistent, and we spoke on several occasions over those few weeks. The calls with my father were sometimes tense and usually short in nature, but both of them let me know they were there if ever I needed them. Neither of them really asked about Terrence, and I knew they were letting me take the lead on that.

I went back to the firm on Monday with a heavy heart. This was supposed to be a happy time for me, but instead I felt burdened. How had I gotten here?

As I was approaching the kitchen to heat my lunch up, I heard Turkey-Neck and another colleague, Neil, speaking lowly. The door wasn't fully closed. I crept over to the cracked door and refused to move as I strained to hear what the two men were saying.

Neil said, "I truly appreciate your assistance in helping me get rid of those cases. They were killing me."

"No problem, Neil. I wish you wouldn't have waited so long. I made sure they were routed to the proper person."

"Whoever gets those cases is going to have quite a job on their hands."

"Oh, it's okay. With a little nudging, Uncle Colin insisted I give it to one of the best attorneys at the firm. She'll make sure to get it handled. She's always trying to prove she's better than me anyway," Bill responded.

Uncle Colin?

Bill continued, "We want to make sure we take good care of you, Neil, and help you get to where you want to go."

"Yes, sir," Neil replied.

His comment prompted me to look up, and I squinted through the door opening just in time to see Bill reach over and put his hand on Neil's shoulder. "Bonnie was the one exception to this rule because she's fucking beautiful and can be very persuasive in the bedroom, if you know what I mean; but this is a man's world, and we're not going to let any woman come in and take our place. Especially not a fat Black one. She thinks she's going to eventually make partner, but not on my watch. Not here, not today, not ever."

They both laughed, and I almost threw up. I couldn't believe my ears. Go figure. Bill was Colin's nephew, and I was right about the one woman who did make partner; she was definitely sleeping with someone. That explained why no matter what I did, I couldn't get ahead. And did I hear him say he's never going to let a fat Black woman become partner? That disgusting, little, racist bastard. I'd been right about him all along! He was setting me up to fail and I had been damn-near killing myself for three and a half years for nothing!

I had to pull myself together before anyone saw me, so I gathered myself and made it back to my office. I was having a hard time catching my breath, my chest was tight, and I was sweating profusely. Dammit, I had to get myself in a gym because this was ridiculous. I'd lost my appetite and needed to get out of there. I grabbed my purse and hightailed it out of the office. The receptionist saw me as I was rushing out the door.

She asked, "Are you okay, Ms. Thompkins?"

I could barely speak, but I nodded and managed to squeak out, "Yes, I'll be back shortly."

"Okay, ma'am," she answered, but I could tell by her tone that my act was not convincing.

When I got to my car, I turned the AC on high and let it blow on me as I took several sips of water to calm myself down. I realized how badly my hands were shaking. I was seriously thinking of quitting at that moment and needed someone to talk me off the ledge, so I dialed Terrence's number.

"Hey, you," he answered.

"Hey, baby. I have to talk to you."

"Of course," he said. "Everything okay?"

"No, nothing is!" I cried. I shared the conversation I'd just heard between Bill and Neil, and how I was ready to quit.

"Wow, I can't believe he said that."

"Me neither! I can't take it anymore. I've given these people too much for them to keep taking advantage of me like this! I'm never going to be able to become partner here."

He answered casually, "Sometimes we have to put up with certain things to get to where we want to go."

I pulled the phone away from my ear and stared at it. Huh? Were we having the same conversation? Did he not hear everything I'd just said? What part of *I'm never going to be able to become partner here* did he not understand?

"I get that, but I'm obviously not going to get anywhere staying at this company, and frankly, I'm tired."

His next reply shocked me. "You're strong, you'll be okay. Besides, you have responsibilities. You can't just quit."

Wow! Just wow! Talk about lack of empathy.

"Never mind. Just forget it, Terrence," I said and hung up on him.

I called Devyn next and let him know what I'd just heard. Like me, he was flabbergasted that Bill and Colin were related, and he wasn't surprised about how Bonnie had become partner or about them blocking me from moving up. "So, you were right about them all along," he acknowledged.

"Yep," I answered.

"Well, you know that's discrimination and we can get them on that," he stated.

"Yeah, but there's no way to prove it."

"I hear you, but we can get proof. You can't just quit. You're too good of an attorney to let them win, Anisa."

I thought about what he said briefly, but my mind was made up. "Look, I hear what you're saying, Devyn, but I'm done." I paused because not only was I thinking of leaving the firm, but I wasn't sure if I was going to practice law anymore, period. I was bored, completely over it. And frankly, I just didn't give a damn anymore. I realized I was hanging around for the wrong reasons, and I wasn't interested in giving those people any more of my energy.

While I spoke to Devyn, Terrence called me several times, but I ignored him. I had no interest in hearing anything his ass had to say.

I got myself something to eat and slowly made my way back to the firm. I decided I would turn in my two-week resignation first thing the next morning. My common sense had kicked in, and although I wanted to walk off my job that day, my structured nature forced me to play it safe. Besides, in this line of business, you never knew if you might need a reference for the next company.

CHAPTER 25

Be Careful What You Ask For

When I got home that evening, after another long day of work, Terrence's car was in my driveway. I sighed because he was the last person I wanted to see that night. When I opened the door, he had several beautiful bouquets throughout the house and my Sea Orchid, candle from The Gift Genie burning. The candle and flowers had my house smelling delicious, and was that food I smelled?

He emerged with one of my aprons on. "Welcome home, lovely lady!"

"Mm-hmm," I muttered as I dropped my bag and files on the chair and side-eyed him.

"I'm sorry that I didn't seem supportive today. I had a rough day as well." He walked over to me and kissed me on my lips.

"Oh, really," I answered dryly. "What happened?"

"Oh, it's okay, beautiful. We can talk about my day later. I want to know about yours."

I wondered what had gotten into him.

"You sure?"

"I'm positive," he replied and kissed me again. He grabbed my hand and pulled me toward the dining table. He pulled out a chair. "Sit."

I did as I was told as he went to the kitchen and came out with two plates with a small piece of salmon and a spoonful of vegetables.

"I realized that you had a long day at work, and I wanted to do something special for you."

"Awww, thanks baby." I smiled.

He put the plate down in front of me, and I stared at it. It looked good, but where was the rest of it?

I continued to stare at the food as I picked my fork up. "Um, thanks, love, this looks awesome, but where's the rest of it?"

"What do you mean?" he asked as he cut into his salmon and put a forkful in his mouth.

"I'm hungry, and this is only a tease."

He reached over and grabbed my hand. "Baby, I want us to start eating healthier. Since we're going to be married, I want you to live a long time. Not to mention, I want you to look beautiful in your dress."

While I appreciated him wanting me to live a long time, I planned to look beautiful in my dress no matter what, so I wasn't sure how I felt about his comment. But I let it slide.

He continued, "And when you're done with that, I have a nice hot bath waiting for us."

I nodded. I guess he won back some cool points with that one.

When we were done eating, he took our plates and told me to get in the tub and that he would be in shortly. He had candles burning and jazz playing when I opened the door. I was impressed and definitely grateful for this, because God knows I was tired.

I undressed and looked at myself in the mirror. I looked like I'd gained a few pounds, so I guessed he was right. I wanted to lose some weight anyway, and there was no better time to do it than before my wedding because I didn't want to look back at my pictures and be disgusted with myself.

I lowered myself into the water and closed my eyes. This was heaven. He came in shortly afterward and got in the tub behind me. I leaned on him and sang along with the track as the music played.

"You have such a beautiful voice, Anisa," he said.

"Thanks, baby," I answered.

As he was washing my neck and back, seemingly in a good mood, I decided this would be a good time to tell him what I decided about my job.

"So," I began. "I made a major decision today, and I just wanted to run it by you."

"Okay, what's that?" he asked as he continued to bathe me.

"I'm turning in my resignation tomorrow morning."

The water splashed, and I realized that he'd dropped the loofah.

"You're doing what?"

I turned around so he could see my face and repeated myself louder and slower so there was no misunderstanding. "I'm resigning tomorrow. I'm giving my two-week notice."

"So, what are *we* going to do?" he asked.

I glared at him because he must've lost his mind. "What do you mean, what are *we* going to do?"

"I'm sorry, baby, I just mean … did you find another job? Are you going to another firm?"

I shook my head. "Well, not that you care, but I plan to take some time off, and I just might pursue some other things."

"Pursue other things! Other things like what?"

"I don't know, Terrence. Maybe a singing career, maybe travel the world some. I'm not sure, but this job is killing me!"

"Anisa, you're a brilliant attorney. Why you would want to leave that is beyond me. Why don't I help you look for other firms? I can talk to my cousin. She knows of several firms and …"

I couldn't believe it. Just a minute ago, he was just telling me how beautiful my voice was, but now all he was worried about was me staying at a job that I hated? Selfish bastard! I cut him off. "I don't want to do this anymore!"

He glared at me. "I can't believe you're doing this to us."

"Doing what? Attempting to be happy?" I fussed as I stared at him in utter disbelief.

"I thought I made you happy!"

I took a few deep breaths to calm myself because there was no reasoning with this man. Again, Terrence was showing me his true colors. My chest was getting tight, and I wasn't going to let him stress me anymore. "You know, the more I think about it, I'm realizing that the only person you care about is yourself. I'm done with this," I said as I began to get out of the tub.

"Wait, no! I apologize," he replied and grabbed my wrist.

I wanted to hurt him again, so one of us had better move. I yanked my arm away. "I need my space. You need to leave."

"Listen, Anisa. I'm sorry. What I wanted to tell you earlier is that I'm stressed as well because they're downsizing at my company, and I think I might be one of the people they let go," he blurted out.

His comment caught me off guard, but I couldn't feel sorry for him in that moment. My mind was already made up about my job, and I didn't care what he had going on. I stepped out of the tub, grabbed my robe, and left him with nothing but bubbles and his thoughts to keep him company.

Our beautiful moment had come to an end.

Although I was disgusted with him, I decided I might be overreacting, so I let Terrence stay the night. I lay awake as he slept beside me, and I stared at my ring as my mind replayed what Zahair had said to me. "I can't love you more than you love you, and I damn sure can't want more for you than you want for yourself." Terrence didn't give me any of that. Right now, I damn sure didn't feel loved, and Terrence never made me feel that he cared about my happiness. In fact, he was downright selfish. I was beginning to see that I really didn't know this man I was getting ready to marry, and if he was the man I was really supposed to be with, why was it Zahair's face that I saw when I closed my eyes at night?

Before Terrence had gone to bed, he had kissed me and said, "If we need to go to counseling to make us work, I'm willing to do just that because I love you."

I told him I loved him, too. But I wasn't sure if that's what I felt for him anymore, and I also wasn't so sure it was counseling that we needed. I had begun asking myself if it was Terrence that I was really in love with. Was it just the idea of marriage?

I also couldn't shake my father's words: "I suggest you take some time out and make sure you know without a shadow of a doubt that it's you he really wants, because we men don't change overnight."

The next morning, before Terrence left, I told him I needed some time to think and I asked him for some space. He didn't like it, but he reluctantly agreed.

"Okay," he said. "I'll call you in a few days."

"Actually, Terrence, I'll call you," I countered.

When he walked out my front door, he turned around to kiss me, but I turned my head slightly and gave him my cheek. He looked as if he wanted to say something, but instead he kissed my cheek and left.

As I drove to work that day, I said aloud, "Lord, I need some answers." I see why they say that you should be careful what you ask for, because it wasn't long before I would get all the confirmation I needed.

CHAPTER 26

So Long, Farewell

The next day, I happily turned in my resignation and spent the next few days attempting to clean up the files I had acquired since one of my colleagues was out on maternity leave. I wanted to make sure they were in working order before I handed them over to the next poor soul. I figured it would probably be Devyn, and because he was my friend, I didn't want him to have to deal with this mess. I had managed to catch up pretty well, and now the files were only a few weeks behind.

Around 10:18 a.m. on this particular morning, I came across a file at the bottom of my dwindling pile. It had the name Asha Atkins on it. *Wow, what a coincidence,* I thought, but I realized this would've been too big of a coincidence. I closed my eyes and prayed that my mind was just playing tricks on me. When I opened my eyes, unfortunately, the name hadn't changed. I opened the file and gasped as I read over the documents:

IN THE CIRCUIT COURT OF THE 11TH COURT FOR MIAMI-DADE COUNTY, FLORIDA, FAMILY DIVISION, IN RE: THE MARRIAGE OF Petitioner (Wife): ASHA L. ATKINS and Respondent (Husband): TERRENCE R. ATKINS **PETITION FOR DISSOLUTION OF MARRIAGE WITH DEPENDENT OR MINOR CHILDREN.**

I skimmed the page for more of the document's contents, especially where it showed the marriage date. May 28, 2017. I slapped my hand over my mouth when I realized they had been married for over two years, which is around the time Mikel was born. Again, I felt myself struggling to breathe and my chest tightening. I took a sip of water to calm myself down and wiped my forehead as I continued to read. Asha's reason for filing: Adultery and Irreconcilable Differences.

I felt lightheaded, and I was sure I was going to faint, so I took another sip of water, closed my eyes, leaned forward, and rested my head on my fingers. Hot tears stung my eyes as my stomach filled with butterflies, but they weren't the good ones. They were the angry-beyond-description butterflies. They were the butterflies that let me know it was a good thing I no longer cared about being an attorney because I was about to lose my law license.

Married! Terrence was married? He had made me into

a hypocrite because I had accused Nia of doing the thing I realized I was also doing. I was sleeping with a married man.

I also realized this divorce petition had been filed right around the time of my birthday, and it hadn't even been a full month since he'd proposed to me. That lying, cheating bastard! If I'd had the slightest doubt that I was done with Terrence, this solidified my decision to leave him for good, but I wasn't going to let him get away that easily.

For a brief second, I thought about calling him and cussing him out, but I figured I'd do one better. Conflict of interest or not, I called the number in the file and waited for her to answer. After the third ring, she picked up.

"Hello?"

"Hello, may I please speak to Asha Atkins?"

"This is she."

"Hi Asha, my name is Anisa Thompkins, and I'm the attorney who is taking over the files from the previous attorney who is now out on maternity leave. I have been assigned to your case for your Petition for Divorce from Terrence Atkins, and I would like to introduce myself as well as go over some things. Would you be available to come into the office either this afternoon or tomorrow at around 10:00 a.m.?"

"Um. Okay. Well, I have some things planned for tomorrow morning, so I think today would work best. Would you be available around 2:30 today?"

Oh, she had no idea how available I would be. "Sure, that would be perfect," I answered. I was going to get all the answers I needed one way or the other.

I don't know how I managed to keep it together as I waited for her arrival, because I was hanging on by a thread. When our receptionist buzzed me to let me know Asha arrived, my heart began to pound.

"Send her in, please," I responded. I took a deep breath and prayed that the line of sweat I felt trailing down my back and pooling in my bra wouldn't leave a stain.

When I heard the knock on my door, I wasn't sure what to expect. *I hope I'm at least cuter than she is,* I thought.

When she poked her head in, I smiled. Like me, she was pretty and fat.

Okay, so his ass definitely has a type, I thought.

I stood up and walked over to shake her hand. "Come in. Have a seat," I told her as I gestured to the chair in front of my desk.

She smiled awkwardly, and I wondered what she was thinking about me.

"Sorry for the last-minute call. It's just that I've been so backed up with cases that I'm just getting to yours and wanted to make sure I spoke to you so we can move forward as soon as possible."

It was partially true, because I knew I wouldn't stay around long enough to work her case.

"No, it's no problem, really," she said, shrugging. "I just want to get Terrence out of my life as soon as possible."

Don't I know it? Me too.

I went down the list of formal questions with her and

braced myself when I asked, "So, you said you wanted to leave Terrence on the grounds of adultery and irreconcilable differences. Would you care to elaborate?"

She sucked her teeth and rolled her eyes. I could tell the homegirl was about to come out. "Terrence's sorry ass," she muttered. She cleared her throat and looked at me. "Oh, excuse me. It's hard to be professional when I talk about him."

I leaned forward and locked eyes with her. "You have nothing to be sorry about," I reassured her. *Hell, God knows he made me cuss on numerous occasions.*

I continued, "I understand. We know that this is a hard time for the parties involved."

She looked down at my ring. "That's a beautiful ring. It looks similar to the one I had. Are you married?"

I glanced down at my ring finger and covered it with my free hand. "Oh. Um, thanks. I'm engaged."

"Okay," she answered. She locked eyes with me. "Marriage can be a wonderful thing when done right, but you just make sure you're marrying the right partner because you don't want to go through what I've been through and end up where I am. You know?"

I wasn't sure if she was trying to reassure herself or me, but I nodded and answered, "I hear you."

She pointed to her chin. "You see this scar?"

Again, I nodded.

"This scar is from when I got into an accident with our son in the car. I was arguing with Terrence about not coming home yet again when I swerved off the road."

I stared at her in pure disbelief. Wow! That was the time

that bastard had called me and told me they were in the hospital. I was going to kill him if I ever saw him again. I realized that although I'd had it bad with Terrence giving me several emotional scars, he had given her both physical and emotional scars in some form. The man was just plain toxic. There was no other way to describe him.

She continued, "Okay, so, where was I?"

The more she spoke, the more nauseated I felt. She shared that Terrence was a liar, preyed on women who had low self-esteem and good jobs, and he cheated throughout their whole marriage.

Damn, damn, and damn. My mouth felt dry, and I silently prayed my face wouldn't give me away. I found my voice. "So, when you said he cheated—"

"Yes, I meant just that. He doesn't have a faithful bone in his body. I think he only married me because I got pregnant with our son, and the only reason he even spoke to me is because he met me at my school and learned I was the school principal, so he realized I was career driven. I think he already had someone when we met, but he told me it was over."

Oh, did he now? I filed that away in my mental rolodex. I continued, "What about the lying? Other than cheating, did he lie about anything else?"

Her eyes got wide. "Did he? Umph! His ass doesn't have a pot to piss in, talking about he was a financial advisor and did real estate. He doesn't own shit! The house we lived in—when he did decide to come home, that is—is mine. The home he lived in when we met is his brother's. His brother basically gave it to him and told him to pay the utilities, and he can barely do that."

I swallowed hard. I felt faint for the umpteenth time today. I fanned myself and said, "Excuse me" as I took a sip of water.

"Are you okay?" she asked.

"Oh yes. I, um, don't think the AC is working properly in my office today."

"Oh. Okay," she answered hesitantly.

I continued, "And how do you know all of this?"

"I probably wouldn't have known if I didn't have my son, but when I was about to have Mikel, I demanded to meet the family that he had left because our son deserved to know his relatives. That family was Terrence's brother and his brother's wife. Thank God they were up front with me as to his dating history, but we were already married by then, so I tried to make it work."

Terrence had a brother? He told me his parents both died in a house fire when he was a child, but he never mentioned any siblings, and I was so blinded by dumb love that I didn't push even when he wouldn't bring me around his son. How dumb could one person be?

My head was throbbing. *Keep it together, Anisa.* "Okay," I answered and wiped my forehead. "One more thing. Do you know the address of his brother's home?"

"Sure, hold on," she said and searched her purse. "I asked his brother for the address because I realized I might need to show he lied about owning the property. I also did a property search. The house is definitely in his brother's name."

She pulled out a piece of paper with the address on it. "Here you are."

I had already figured it out, but I needed to see it with my own two eyes. When I looked at the address, not surprisingly, it was the same house I'd been going to when I went to *his* house.

I let her finish getting out everything she needed to and then asked if she had signed a prenuptial agreement.

"That's the one smart thing I did before I married him. I worked too hard to get what I have, even though he fought me tooth and nail not to get one. Even with that, I've already lost so much. He's basically drained most of my savings, and I don't even know how I'm going to pay for all this court stuff, but that's okay. I'll do whatever I have to do to get rid of his ass."

I'm sure he did fight that prenup. That sorry bastard. I breathed a sigh of relief that she had at least taken that precaution. "Okay, make sure you send that over as well, so we can look over the terms."

"Okay." She nodded.

I hated that I couldn't try to get him to pay the court costs because he had no real income. The most I could do was see if she could get child support. I felt sorry for this woman. She reminded me a lot of myself because she was so trusting, and she wanted to be loved so much that she ignored all of the signs.

"Okay, so since he doesn't have anything for you to get, I can look to see if there is something we can get him on."

She leaned forward and locked eyes with me again. "The

only thing I want is full custody and to get on with my life. It's not like he's a good father, anyway. He's barely home because he's out running the street with God knows who. He only started trying to do better when I threatened to divorce him."

Damn. That who *is probably me.* I shook my head again. "Okay, well if you don't have any additional questions, thanks for your time. I'm going to look everything over and get back to you shortly. I don't want to make any promises, but we may be able to at least get you custody, especially with him being an absentee father."

She put her hand on mine, and I thought I saw tears in her eyes.

"Thank you. Thank you so much," she said. She got up to leave and I walked her to the door. Before she walked out of my office, she turned around and shook my hand again. I felt guilty for doing things this way, but I was definitely going to make sure her case got into the right hands when I left.

Everything now made complete sense. So, Terrence came back to me because Asha was divorcing him, and he figured I was someone who could take care of him. That's why he acted crazy the other night when I told him I was quitting. He had played on my low self-esteem, and to top it off, he'd been lying to me all of this time about almost everything. He wouldn't let me meet his son because he probably wasn't with him on those nights he said he was, or better yet, he was probably with Asha. Three years of my life! I felt sick.

How I was an attorney and never once thought to vet his ass was beyond me, but I recognized that when we women loved, sometimes we overlooked things. Or maybe I wanted the M-word so much that I saw in him exactly what I wanted to see. I wasn't sure, but what I did know was that everyone was right about him. Payback was in order, and I wanted to whoop his ass for every year I let him take from me.

When Asha was gone, I put her number in my phone then dialed the number of the person (other than my father and Talia) who I knew wanted to beat Terrence down as much as I now did. She answered on the first ring.

"Hey, Mo," I said. "Are you busy? I think I'm finally going to take you up on that drive by."

CHAPTER 27

Ready for War

She met me at my house at 7:30 that night. When Monique arrived, she had on a full camouflage outfit and a cap that read "Ready For War." She had black paint under her eyes, and she was wearing army boots. I knew she was wild, but I had never seen her quite like this. Anyone could tell she had done this a time or two in her lifetime because when she walked in, she had a black duffle bag filled with all kinds of shit. She dropped it on the floor.

"What's that for?" I asked.

"You wouldn't go into a battle without your weaponry, right?" She bent down, opened the bag, and pulled out a tire iron, a wrench, a hammer, tape, a rope, an army knife, and some other stuff that I couldn't decipher.

"Monique, we're just going to drive by his house to confront him."

"You might be just trying to drive by, but I'm going to wreck shop." She sat down on the couch and looked at her nails. "I'm glad I didn't get my manicure yet."

I'd given her the rundown of what I'd found out that day at work, and how I called Asha to get the dirt, and it didn't take her long to get to my house. She'd been waiting for this day for a long time. "I would've done the same thing," she told me.

That's what I was afraid of. I examined my outfit: jeans, a white T-shirt, and some sneakers. "What do you think about what I have on?"

She studied me. "Well, if you don't care about getting blood on it, then I would keep it on. If not, throw on some sweats or something. Just make sure whatever you have on, you can bob and weave in it."

She must have seen the exasperated look on my face, so she added, "Girl, I'm just fuckin' with ya. Now hurry up!"

I was beginning to reconsider if calling Monique was a such a good idea after all. "Um, okay, give me a sec."

I went back to my room and put on some black sweats and a cap. I looked in the mirror. Much better.

I wasn't feeling well. I was sweating again, and I felt nauseous.

"I feel like I'm going to throw up and my heart is racing," I told her.

She waved it off. "Oh, chile, that's just your nerves. You'll be fine. You ready?"

"I guess," was all I could muster.

We got in her car, and she explained how we would go about everything as we drove. "We're going to park across the street and post up, and then you call him and tell him you're outside and when he comes out …"

I couldn't hear what she was saying after a while. I felt like I was in an episode of Charlie Brown. "Whomp, whomp, whomp whomp whomp," was all I heard. My heart palpitated and my hands became clammy and shakier the closer we got to his house.

When we pulled up, Monique turned her headlights off and parked. I didn't see anything out of the ordinary other than the third car in the driveway as I knew he only owned two—if they were even really his.

As Monique and I sat across the street from the house, I asked myself, *How did I get here?* I was supposed to be the good girl, the straight-laced sister, the one who got straight A's, stayed a virgin until I was twenty-two, and got a career doing what I thought would give prestige and make me look good, but here I was doing what I promised myself I would never do.

We sat for a few moments while Jazmine Sullivan's "Bust Your Windows" played in the background. Finally, Monique said, "Dial his number and see if he'll come outside."

"And say what?" I asked.

She shrugged and spoke with her hands. "I don't know! This is your loser! Tell him you're dropping off a package or something."

I dialed his number, but he didn't pick up. I said, "He didn't answer."

"Try again," she ordered as she watched the house.

Again, I did as I was told. "Still no answer," I said again.

"Hmm, well his ass is definitely home. I can see shadows in the window."

I seriously began to think about what I was doing. I was supposed to be done with him, so why was I even doing this?

"I've changed my mind. He's just not worth it."

She gestured to the ring I was still wearing. "Doesn't look like you're done to me."

She was right. My mouth said I was done, but I still left a small window open for him to come back, even after all the mess he was putting me through, and me wearing his ring proved it. I'd let my desire for marriage take over my good sense.

Just as I was about to respond, his front door opened and a woman came out. He followed, laughing and holding her hand.

"Is that her?" Monique asked.

I guess I wasn't done, because I got angry all over again when I realized the woman he was with wasn't even his ex-wife-to-be. "Oh, hell nah," I fussed as I grabbed the door handle. All of my hesitancy went out the window, and I was about to beat the black off him.

I stopped for a second. My heart was pounding rapidly, and it felt like a furnace ignited inside of my body. I pulled at the neck of my sweatshirt, fanned myself with my hand, and said, "Mo, turn up the AC."

She glanced over at me. "Damn, girl, it's already on the highest setting. You 'bout to have me turn into a popsicle up in here. You okay?"

Hell no! "I think so," I lied, but the doors of the car felt like they were closing in on me.

After a brief moment of hand fanning and checking to make sure the air vents were aimed at me, I began to feel weak. "Mo," I whispered.

"Yeah?" she answered without her eyes ever leaving Terrence and his mystery woman.

"I can't breathe."

"What?" she asked, now giving me her full attention.

I used my last bit of strength to gasp, "I—can't—breathe … Hospital!"

Her anger quickly turned to worry as a look of terror ran across her face. "Oh my God, oh my God!" she replied frantically. "Okay, hold on, my friend!" She started the car and took off.

I felt the car swerve a few times to the left and the right as she drove like a madwoman to get me to a hospital. The last thing I remember was her calling my name.

"Anisa! Anisa!

CHAPTER 28

Panic No More

When I woke up, I heard machines beeping. I opened my eyes and looked around slowly, but it didn't take a genius to recognize where I was.

My mother's face was the first one I saw. "Hey, queen." She smiled and rushed over to hug me.

I was too happy to see her.

I spotted my father next. "Daddy! What happened?" I asked.

He came over, leaned down, and kissed my forehead. "You're going to be okay, princess. It was just a severe panic attack."

A panic attack? That's it? I couldn't believe it. It felt like I was about to die.

The doctor emerged. "How's the patient?"

"I'm okay, I think," I replied as I began to sit up.

"Hold on," Iya said as she hit the button to adjust my bed.

The doctor smiled. "We think you'll be just fine, but we wanted to run some tests before we sent you home."

"Panic attack?" I asked. "I was having a hard time breathing, I felt lightheaded, and my heart was beating fast."

"Yes, and you passed out, too. Panic attacks as severe as the one you had can mimic the symptoms of a heart attack. It looks like you may be suffering from anxiety. Tell me, have you ever experienced those symptoms before?"

"Well, over the past week or so. Minus the passing out," I answered.

"Okay," he replied and wrote something in his notepad. "And what about stress? Have you been under any added stress lately?"

I chuckled. That was an understatement. I thought about the last few months of my life. I'd broken up with someone whom I thought loved me, had the time of my life in DC, reconnected with a man who genuinely seemed to love me, had the best sex of my life with him, stopped speaking to him, entered a new decade of life and discovered my true passion with singing, got proposed to, disappointed my family to the point that they were barely speaking to me, received confirmation that the people at my job had it out for me and were setting me up to fail, quit my job, found out the man who proposed to me was a married fraud, went and did a stakeout in front of his house, and then had a severe panic attack.

At this point, anyone would agree I was lucky that's all it was, and I was secretly thankful that I'd gotten the panic attack when I did because only God knows what would've happened if Monique and I ran up on Terrence. The one thing I did know without a shadow of a doubt was that he wasn't worth it, and I was done.

"Yes," I answered. "I have a whole lot going on with my job and relationship at the moment."

"Mm-hmm," the doctor said as he nodded and wrote that down as well. "Well, let's get some blood from you so we can send it to the lab, and we'll just keep you tonight for observation. How does that sound?"

It didn't sound good because I hated hospitals, but I responded, "Okay."

When he left, Monique poked her head in the door. "Can I come in?"

"Of course, you can," my mother answered. She waved her in.

Monique came in and smiled at me. "You scared me half to death. I'm so glad you're okay," she said and hugged me.

"Me too." I smiled.

Shortly after, Talia arrived along with Nia.

"Hey there," Talia said. She hugged me tight and held on to me longer than necessary.

"I'm so sorry," I said, crying.

She shook her head. "No, sis. I'm sorry. I should've never told you what you should be doing with your life. You can make your own decisions, not to mention I don't know what I would've done if something would've happened to you and we never had the chance to speak again."

Nia then hugged me. "I'm glad you're okay, too."

We smiled at each other and that's one of the first times in a long time that I felt that her words were genuine.

"What the hell happened anyway?" Nia asked.

My parents looked at me curiously as well when she asked.

I glanced at Monique, and she looked back at me, and we started laughing. "Um, that's a story for another time."

Talia glanced at us and gave the all-knowing look. She laughed as well because I was pretty sure Monique had filled her in as to our whereabouts when all of this went down.

At that moment, I realized the people who genuinely loved and cared about me were all in the room. The only person missing was Jamie.

Before the doctor gave me the green light to be released the next morning, he informed me that my lab results had come back. "Your blood pressure was elevated when you came in, which was no surprise due to the panic attack, but it seems to be normal again. For the most part, your labs are good, but your cholesterol is higher than I would like it to be. Also, I know diabetes runs in your family, and I want you to get everything under control so you don't become diabetic as well. I would also like for you to watch out for stressors in your life and monitor your blood pressure. If you experience symptoms like you did yesterday, I want you to come back in, so we can figure out if we need to give you something for anxiety. I'm not going to put you on any meds right now, but if you don't get your stress under control, we'll have to look into other options. I suggest you make a few dietary changes, and I have a few pamphlets that can show you what you should be eating to help with lowering your cholesterol. They also show some deep breathing exercises to help keep your stress levels in check."

"Okay, doc," I told him. "The next time I see one of you doctors again, it'll be for you to tell me how perfect all of my numbers are."

"That's what I like to hear," he answered and gave me the thumbs up.

My mother was the queen of healthy living, but I didn't bother to tell him that. I knew she'd be ecstatic to help me out with a lifestyle overhaul, and I wanted to try it without any meds first, so I was determined to get my health in order. The first step was getting rid of unnecessary stress. That meant getting rid of Terrence for good.

First, I called my father and asked him to change my locks immediately and let me know when it was done. He gladly obliged, and it was done in no time. He didn't ask me much, but he knew the deal. While lying up in the hospital, I'd made the decision that going forward, I was choosing me and no longer giving my energy to anyone who didn't deserve it.

I sent Terrence a simple text: "I've decided that it's over. Don't attempt to contact me, because your privileges have now been revoked. Have a nice life, or not." I figured that would drive him crazy, kind of like I'd almost allowed myself to go crazy over him. Some might've argued it wasn't cool since we were supposedly engaged, and it might've been extreme considering how long we'd dated, but I was finally resolute on my dealings with him. I looked down at my finger, slipped the ring off, and put it in the pocket of my purse. Then I hit the block option under his name on my phone. I shrugged and muttered, "Hey, men break up with women over text all the time."

As far as the healthy eating went, I was going to get started the next day, but that day, I was going to grab some three cheese mac and cheese with crab, shrimp, and scallops from iSeefood when I got out of the hospital.

When I got home, I went around my house packing up anything that belonged to Terrence or reminded me of him. I wanted to pull a *Waiting to Exhale* and burn all his shit up, but I figured it would be best if someone else got some use out of it, so I made two piles. All of his expensive designer stuff (hopefully it was real, being that everything else about him was fake) I put in one bag. I decided that those things would mysteriously end up on his and Asha's doorstep—maybe she'd want to sell it and make some additional income.

Everything else, I put in the other bag. Those things would go to Monique and Talia so they could take it to their churches and sell them at the church fundraiser. Oh, he was going to be pissed when he found out.

Perfect! I thought.

After a few days, his calls began to come in. One by one at first, and then they became more frequent. Of course, I couldn't receive them, but I got all of his voicemails.

Day 1: "Wait, did you block me? Anisa?"

Day 2: "What did I do to deserve this?" and "Anisa, how could you just give up on us like this?"

Day 3: "Anisa, I miss you" and "I'm coming by tonight if I don't hear from you soon" and "Are you okay?"

Day 4: "Anisa? Anisa?" and "I can't believe you would do this to us" and "What could I have done that was so bad for you to just stop talking to me? And over text, really, Anisa?"

Day 5: "You're really pissing me off, Anisa" and "Well at least let me come and get my shit" and "Anisa, stop playing!" and "I love you, baby. Don't do this."

Day 6: "Anisa, what's going on? This is just ridiculous." Then some heavy breathing. And, "I was the only one who wanted you, and this is how you treat me?"

And there it was. This time, his words didn't hurt me, though, because I knew his words weren't true. Even if they were, I would've been happier rotting on an island all by myself than dealing with his ass ever again. If he did manage to slip in through my guard gate and show up at my home, I'd let him know I had all his messages saved, and I would file a restraining order for harassment if he didn't leave me alone. It felt good to finally take back some control of my life.

Oh, and don't think he didn't try to contact me via other methods (email, unknown numbers), but I knew better than to answer because we all know that when we ladies are fed up … I'll let you complete the rest of that statement.

It was an added bonus that I didn't need to show my ass to make a point. I discovered that sometimes there was nothing like silence to say everything that needed to be said.

CHAPTER 29

How You Like Me Now?

I hurried through the airport because I wanted to get to the hospital as soon as possible. Talia had just given birth, and I was anxious to see my new niece. She had gone into labor a week early, but we were all relieved because her pregnancy hormones were making her miserable as hell.

It was amazing how thinking you were going to die could change the way you viewed the world. It had been three months since I'd left my job and had that horrible panic attack, and I was envisioning where I could go for my next trip. I'd taken Iya's advice and gone on several trips during this time. Iya and I thought it would be amazing to go somewhere in Africa next. Maybe a mother–daughter kind of thing.

My first trip was to New York to see Jamie because she had decided to move back home to DC and was in the process of packing. Her lease would be up shortly. She said she would stay with her parents while she and Tyrone continued to date, and she wouldn't move in with him until there was a ring on her finger. It was old school, but I was glad she'd chosen to stick by her beliefs, and I couldn't say I blamed her to do it that way.

After that, I wanted to go someplace warm and visit an island that I'd never been to before, so I chose the Virgin Islands because I almost froze to death in New York. I was ready to live boldly, so I took a five-day cruise by myself. My friends thought I was crazy, but I was able to meet a few people on the ship, and I had the time of my life. It gave me time to reflect and rediscover who I really was.

There was so much good happening for me in such a short amount of time that my head was spinning. Several days after I left my job at the firm, the idea to open my own nonprofit came to mind. I ran it by Devyn, and it didn't take long before he called and told me he'd found a space, and the rent was perfect if I was interested in taking over the office space. I didn't waste time giving him the deposit, and within a month and a half, we were about to be up and running.

My nonprofit was the miracle I never saw coming. I knew without a shadow of a doubt that I was making the right decision about opening Iya's Gems, and a month later Devyn had also quit the firm to help out. Now, we were going to be partners of the organization. We knew each other's work ethic, so we knew we would be dedicated to the organization, and we both wondered why we'd never thought of this before.

When I got to the hospital, my family was all there: Dad, Dad's new girlfriend, Iya, Adebayo, Nia, and Darius. Adebayo greeted me and left the room so that the room wouldn't be crowded.

I could tell Talia was tired, but her face lit up when she saw me. "Hey, sis!" she exclaimed as she held her new baby. "Come check out your niece."

I smiled and went over to her. I stared down at her bundle of joy. She was perfect, and I think I already picked up a hint of Talia in her eyes. She opened her little mouth and made a sound.

"Hey, sis," I said and hugged Talia carefully.

I glanced up in time to see Nia staring at me. She looked as if she'd put on a few pounds. This was the thickest I'd ever seen her. The extra weight looked good on her, and her butt was even bigger than before.

She smiled at me, and I smiled back. She and I had grown much closer after my panic attack, and she informed me that she found the courage to finally step out on her own and leave her no-good husband, and that I was her inspiration. I was amazed and touched by her revelation. She also revealed she was jealous of me at times. Her reason: I effortlessly got good grades in school. I barely had to study to get straight A's while she had to work her ass off to get B's. She also envied my relationship with Iya. You couldn't tell her I wasn't Iya's favorite because of our singing bond. This was further confirmation that no matter how good something looked on the outside, everyone had something they were insecure about.

Her biggest revelation, though, was that the new man in her life was a good guy and although she may have gone about being with him the wrong way, she was glad she'd met him because he treated her how she'd always desired to be treated. The most exciting thing was that she was pregnant again and expecting a baby in about six months. In the interim, we realized that it wasn't her who couldn't have children, but her ex-husband to be. This time, she'd made it through the first trimester, so she felt okay telling everyone about her pregnancy. So, as horrible as it might sound, if she never stepped out of her marriage, she probably never would have known that she could have children. I took that as a valuable lesson to never stay in something that isn't meant for you, because you could miss out on your blessing. I also found out that Jamie was right—Nia didn't want to tell me about her first pregnancy because she didn't want to hurt my feelings.

I was finally becoming whole, and I knew that even if I didn't lose another pound, I was still amazing right where I was.

A few weeks after starting Iya's Gems—my nonprofit for helping girls gain confidence—around 4:00 one afternoon, I heard a knock at my door. Devyn jumped up. "I'm about to leave, you want me to get it?"

"Thanks, sure," I answered without looking up. The girls were already gone for the day, but I figured one of them could've come back to get something they'd forgotten.

I heard a woman and Devyn speaking at the door, and she said, "It's nice to meet you, Devyn." The familiar sound of her voice had me look up in astonishment. She was the last person I expected to see here.

"Hello, Anisa," she said.

"Asha?" I said as I stood up. "Wow! What are you doing here?" She looked good, and she looked much happier than when I'd seen her the last time.

She walked over to my desk. "May I sit?" she asked, gesturing to the chair in front of me.

"Oh, of course," I replied.

She sat down, and I sat back down as well.

We were both silent for a moment. She spoke first. "I know you're probably wondering why I'm here and how I found you."

I nodded.

"Well, I wanted to say thank you."

I wasn't sure what she was talking about, so I asked, "For what?"

"Well, first I wanted to say thank you for the care package." She winked. "I was able to get some extra money by selling Terrence's items on Poshmark and Ebay."

I chuckled uncomfortably.

"Secondly, I want to say thanks for your help with my case."

I had gotten her one of the best divorce attorneys in

Florida after I left the firm and had even given her some money to help out with Asha's case. Not that I owed Asha anything, and I knew it wasn't my fault, but I guess my conscience wouldn't let me leave her high and dry now that I knew I'd been with her husband. This was my way of giving back in some kind of way.

"I'm glad I could help," I said.

"Oh yes, my attorney has been awesome! We're still in court now, and I can get full custody being that I'm the breadwinner and he's been pretty much a deadbeat for most of Mikel's life." She paused. "But I don't really want to keep Mikel away from his father, so I told her to see if he does better on a trial basis, and we can go from there."

Wow, this was one hell of a woman right here. I nodded my head again. "Okay, well if that's what you choose."

"Yes, it is. I was hurt for a long time, but I realized that me staying mad at Terrence wouldn't be good for any of us."

"I can understand that."

She paused and looked around. "This is really awesome. I love what you're doing with these young women."

I looked around in admiration at the center as well. "Thanks. Yes, it's a labor of love for me. Honestly, these young ladies are actually the ones giving me something by becoming their best selves. I wish I would've done this years ago."

She nodded, and we sat in silence for a few moments.

She continued, "I guess you want to know how I knew it was you who dropped those things off and how I found you, right?"

I knew finding me wouldn't be hard because all she had to do was look my name up and my organization would come up.

She continued before I could answer, "Well, when I saw you at the firm that day, you looked strangely familiar. I couldn't remember from where exactly, but I realized I'd seen a picture of you at Terrence's house in a drawer when we first started dating."

I lowered my eyes.

"Then I saw you on my camera when you dropped the items off on my doorstep. Even though you had on the cap and sunglasses, I could make you out right away." She smiled. "And let me say, you might be a wonderful attorney, but you suck at being stealthy."

We both cracked up because she was right.

I finally spoke. "This whole thing could've gone horribly wrong if we were different women. If I knew he was married …"

She shook her head and reached over and put her hand on mine. "Nope, we're not going to do that. We both trusted the wrong man, and truth be told, I knew he had someone when we started messing around. I guess in my heart of hearts, I hoped that once we got married and had a family, that would somehow change him into being faithful. The only person to blame here is Terrence." She rolled her eyes. "Well, and maybe us for not doing background checks on his sorry ass."

We both laughed.

She continued, "We women need to stick together. I'm

not the kind of woman to confront the woman first, because I know better. *He* was my husband, *he* was the one who lied, and *he* was the one who broke up our family. Case closed."

I was speechless. She was a better woman than I was, because I don't know if I could've handled the situation as well as she did.

We became silent again. There wasn't much left to say, because she'd pretty much said it all.

She said, "Well, let me go."

We both got up and I walked her to the door. She paused and looked back at me before she went outside. "And just so you know, I would've done the same thing to get info, too. I want you to know your secret is safe with me."

She was referring to how I called her into my office, even after I found out who she was. I nodded because I could've gotten into some serious trouble over that situation. "I appreciate that."

Her next words caught me off guard. "And to think, all this for a man who didn't even go down on me."

My eyes widened because I didn't know what to say to that.

"Maybe one day, we can grab a drink or something," she offered.

I nodded. That was just weird. I wasn't sure if I was ready for all of that yet, but I replied, "We might be able to do that," and left it at that.

EPILOGUE

I is Married Now!

Today was a beautiful day for a wedding. We were at the Running Hare Vineyard in Maryland, the sun was out, and there was not a cloud in the sky. The weather was warm for Maryland in May, but my Florida blood was thankful.

I peeked out at the crowd as they were arriving. There was a good amount of people, but it wasn't overcrowded, and everyone looked beautiful. I spotted Iya, Adebayo, Talia, Darius, and Nia in the audience. Nia was anxious to get back to the hotel where her boyfriend and baby were and had just left for a few hours so she could be at the wedding. I'd judged her harshly before, but she was actually a better mother than I could've ever anticipated. Talia, on the other hand, had gotten Darius's sister to keep her two daughters for the weekend, and although she loved her girls to death, she couldn't get away fast enough. Darius still wanted his boy, but Talia said she was done. I guess we had to see what would happen with that in the next few years.

It was a production in the room where we ladies were getting prepped. The smell of burned hair was in the air as our hair was getting pressed and curled. The ladies were frantically running back and forth, trying to be ready for the 2:00 ceremony, but we honestly knew we wouldn't be ready on time. *Who's getting their makeup done next? Where are my shoes? The veil is crushed, can someone please run the steamer over it? Did you remember to put on your garter belt?* It was madness, but I welcomed it. My stomach was in knots because I'd be singing a song during the ceremony as well, and I wanted it to be perfect.

I prayed I would make it down the aisle without tripping, and I hoped my deodorant would be giving me my money's worth because I was already beginning to perspire.

I had lost thirty-five pounds in total and was amazed at how good I felt. When I went back to the doctor to check my numbers, he was surprised and impressed by how quickly I had gotten everything in order. I was proud of myself, because it wasn't always an easy feat watching what I ate and staying active, but I now put the same effort and determination I put into my work life into my health. I had also cut back on eating meat and found several delicious food places to satiate my appetite. Surprisingly, I was able to find plenty of delicious vegan options as well, but I still ate the food I liked when I had the taste for it. I just knew I couldn't do it every day.

I was working on my album and debated on forming my

own band, but for now, I had become an honorary member of my mother's band, and I sang with them on several occasions. I had to admit that although my nervousness didn't go away, I wasn't afraid to get on stage anymore. I would find a person in the crowd who I could tell was enjoying my music and concentrate on them or close my eyes for a few seconds if I did feel the nervousness taking over. I had never been so happy in my life, and I knew the best was still yet to come.

After the other women made their way down the aisle, it was finally my turn. I slowly began my walk to the front as the tears formed in my eyes. When I saw his face, I smiled. He was looking handsome as ever with his dreads pulled back into a neat braid and his face cleanly shaven. He looked even more youthful this way, but in my eyes, he could never do wrong in the looks department because he'd always be the handsome king that I fell for. He had on a tuxedo and bow tie and was so damn sharp, he didn't need a knife to cut me. The closer I got to the front, the harder my heart pounded, and I hoped I didn't vomit. When I finally made it to the front, I took several deep breaths and picked up the microphone before the music started.

The instrumental for Amel Larrieux's "Make Me Whole" came through the speakers, and I closed my eyes and let the tears fall as I hit each note perfectly. When I opened my eyes, I fought to keep my composure so my voice didn't crack.

My friend looked stunning as she made her way down the aisle with her father, and Tyrone couldn't help but wipe his eyes as he saw his beautiful bride coming to meet him. Jamie was finally marrying her Prince Charming. It didn't take long for Tyrone to pop the question after she'd moved to DC. He was a smart man because he realized that she was who he wanted, so he didn't waste time locking her down. I guess it's true what they say: when you know, you just know.

When I was done singing, I made my way to my maid-of-honor spot beside her. Jamie had told me she knew it was a lot to ask with me being her maid of honor and performing a song, but she wouldn't dream of having anyone else sing her wedding song, and I was more than happy to oblige.

Zahair was Tyrone's best man, and I hadn't spoken to him since the night he blocked my call. I was tempted on several occasions to reach out, but thank goodness for my work keeping me preoccupied.

The beautiful couple exchanged their vows and exchanged their rings as we all waited anxiously for the pastor to finally announce them as husband and wife and see them kiss and jump the broom. I caught Zahair's eye several times as we stood there, but both of us pretended not to notice each other. I found it funny that the two of us ended up being matched together to walk out. Jamie must've conveniently set that up.

When it was time for us to walk out, I walked over on wobbly legs and tried to play it off. When I touched him to link my arm through his, I felt the electricity shoot through me, and my stomach flip-flopped. I could tell he felt it as well because he paused briefly and, for the first time since I'd seen him that day, he made full eye contact with me.

We went back in to take pictures while the crowd was escorted to where the reception would be held, and more tense moments followed. I felt him watching me, but every time I looked over at him, he would look away. I was no better and did the same thing. We were acting like two big kids. Obviously, I wasn't the only one who noticed because Monique came over to me at one point, rolled her eyes, and asked, "What the hell are y'all doing? Just go over there and talk to him already."

I laughed nervously, but my stubbornness wouldn't let me do anything.

When we got to the reception hall, we lined up outside to walk in arm in arm again and Zahair could no longer help himself. He looked down at me and said, "You look absolutely gorgeous."

Man, I thought. I wanted to rip his clothes off right then and there, but I blushed and cheesed. "Thank you, Zahair. You look very handsome yourself."

The reception was a ball. Everyone did their tributes, and when it was time for them to toss the bouquet, I knew I'd be standing in line as always. Jamie did the ole fake-me-out toss twice, but I didn't move, and when she finally did toss the bouquet behind her, it landed right in my hands. I didn't even have to try.

When it was time for the guys to catch the garter, Zahair was the first one to get on the floor; Monique and Talia nudged me as we laughed. If I remembered correctly, wasn't this the same man who said he disliked garter tosses? When the garter was tossed and all the men stood around watching as it hit the ground, he gladly picked it up, twirled it around his pointer finger, and winked at me.

We'd thrown back several drinks by the time it was time for him to put the garter on. You would've thought he was the groom the way he put that thing in his mouth and slid it up my leg as the crowd screamed and clapped with the show he was putting on. Of course, that just turned me on further. When he was done, he grabbed both my hands and helped me out of the chair. He hugged me and whispered, "Can I talk to you after this?"

My heart pitter-pattered, and I squeaked out a meager, "Sure, okay."

I didn't want to get my hopes up because I didn't know what he had to say, but just getting the chance to speak to him after all this time made me feel giddy. When the reception was almost over and Jamie and her new groom were getting ready to leave, I hugged my friend and her husband. "Enjoy your honeymoon." I winked and added, "And don't come back pregnant."

They had stopped having sex six months before their ceremony, and with the way Jamie was cheesing, I hoped Tyrone had hit the gym recently because she was about to wear his ass out.

We bridesmaids began to do our part in packing up the tablecloths and putting up the centerpieces as Zahair and the other groomsmen went around stacking up the chairs and pulling the garbage cans. Every time I looked up, his eyes were following me. I blushed for the hundredth time that evening. I hadn't had none in a while, so I really needed him to stop looking at me like that.

When we were done and getting ready to leave for the

night, Monique and I hugged goodbye, she left with her boo, and we agreed to meet up the next day for breakfast and to ride to the airport the next evening.

The majority of us were staying at a Marriot in DC, and I was exhausted and wanted to just shower and relax. My family was ready to go and when Iya came over and asked me if I was ready, I told her I'd be right there. Zahair caught me packing up to leave and came over.

He asked, "How long are you here for?"

This felt like déjà vu. "I'll be leaving tomorrow evening."

"Okay. Do you have any plans for tonight?"

"Just relaxing. It's been a long weekend."

He smiled and showed his pearlies. "You're right about that."

We stood in awkward silence before he asked, "Are you staying at the Marriot on Pennsylvania Ave as well?"

I nodded.

"Well, if you don't mind, can I take you?"

I welcomed that. "Sure, I'd like that."

As he drove, we caught up. I was happy to know that both of us were still single.

He surprised me when he said, "So, I saw you on Norah's 'It's in Your Soul Sunday.' I was blown away by how beautiful you looked, and all you've done since the last time we spoke."

He was referring to the interview I'd done with a prominent media personality that had aired the month before. I raised my eyebrows and sat speechless because I didn't know he was even checking for me like that anymore.

He continued, "So you finally left the firm, your nonprofit is thriving, you're modeling, *and* you're singing, huh?"

I found it crazy that I was following in Jamie's footsteps and doing the one thing Auntie Jackie said I could never do. Never in my wildest dreams would I have seen this coming. In all actuality, the one thing I initially hated most about myself turned out to be the catalyst to push me into modeling. The body I tried to cover up for so long was now highly sought after and was a money maker for me. Although I didn't set out to model, my message of self-esteem and self-love had the agencies looking for me.

The modeling I did was mostly for catalog, and it was really more of a hobby for me, but I was glad I could be an example for us thick girls. Chenese Lewis, Denise Bidot, and Lizzo were a just a few of my plus-size role models in the industry. I recently did photo shoots for several Black-owned clothing Brands, and don't think I wasn't waiting for Rihanna to call so I could do a little something something for Fenty.

"Yes. You and my iya were right all along. I honestly didn't know I could ever feel this fulfilled in life. I finally realized that a life without purpose is like drowning and gasping for air. When you find your purpose, you can finally breathe."

He nodded. "Pretty deep stuff. I see that you get it now … Feels good, huh?"

I nodded. "It feels absolutely amazing!"

We sat at the stop light in silence, and he glanced over at me and smiled ever so slightly before he continued, "And don't think I don't see you losing all this weight. You look beautiful, but just know I thought you were beautiful before."

I blushed. "Thanks, Zahair. I know you did. I stopped focusing on the scale and changed up my lifestyle after my panic attack, and with that, the weight started coming off. Iya and I walk a lot, and she even has me doing yoga."

He nodded again, but he didn't take his eyes off me when he said, "Well, I'm proud of you. For everything. You're practically glowing."

The way he looked at me took me back to our college days where he kissed me for the first time in that dingy dorm room. It reminded me why I fell in love with him in the first place. I nodded and felt myself getting lost in his gaze. I diverted my eyes momentarily and answered, "I guess that's what true happiness can bring."

We listened to his radio play for a while before I rested my hand on his and glanced back over at him while he drove. "I just wanted to say thanks for believing in me even when I didn't believe in myself."

He smiled and answered, "I saw your beauty even if you couldn't."

I nodded, but I couldn't bite my tongue. "The only thing I want to know was, how you could walk away from us so easily? I mean, if you believed in me and loved me as you said you did, how could you block my number and not even call once in all this time?"

He glanced at me. "It wasn't easy, Anisa. I threw myself

into my work because I was ready to love you in a way you weren't ready to receive. The only thing that kept me going was when Tyrone would give me updates."

I was surprised because Jamie had never mentioned it. "Wait, you asked about me?"

He pulled up in front of the Marriot, parked, turned off the engine, and turned to face me. "Of course! I even thought to reach out, but then I heard that you had gotten engaged."

Wow! I hoped he hadn't heard about that, but I couldn't be mad. That wasn't something I expected would stay a secret forever.

I lowered my eyes. "Yeah, that."

He chuckled. "Well I'm glad you never went through with it, because from what I heard, the brother left a lot to be desired."

I rolled my eyes. "You ain't never lie!"

We stared at each other for a moment. He finally made his move. "May I walk you to your room?"

I nodded and he got out, walked around, opened my door, and grabbed my hand to help me up. That was my Zahair—always the gentlemen.

When we got my room, he stopped at the front door.

I looked back at him. "Aren't you coming?"

"I don't want you to feel obligated."

I leaned up and kissed him. "Believe me, I don't."

I quickly forgot how exhausted I was, and we stayed up for hours catching up about any and everything that had transpired over the course of us being apart. The next morning, I woke up in his arms. There was no sex; we just spent the rest of the night talking about the direction we saw our lives headed in. It wasn't easy, and as much as we wanted each other, I wanted us to make sure we knew what we were going to do before sex could cloud our judgment.

Us not having sex wasn't a religious thing for me—it was spiritual. Before we went to sleep, Zahair recited some of the beautiful poetry he'd written when we were apart, and he even told me several of the poems were written with me in mind. There was one that was even named after me. He called it "Anisa's Blues." It was about how he wished he could take away my pain because his love for me was insane. Yeah, I know it was a little corny, but it was sweet to me.

Before we fell asleep, he asked, "Do you see yourself being able to build with me, Anisa?"

I absolutely could, but I didn't want to be foolish and jump into anything again, especially if he wasn't willing to do what it took to see the relationship through. I contemplated his question, and I honestly didn't know what I should be doing because there was no right or wrong answer.

I played Iya's words over and over in my head: *rules are meant to be broken*. I could rent my home out if I decided to eventually move to DC, but now I also had Iya's Gems and I wouldn't up and leave my girls just like he wouldn't up and leave his son. We'd just have to see, but for now, I would have to choose me.

The next morning, we hit up Kitchen Cray in Maryland before I had to catch my flight back home, and when Zahair kissed me and told me that he would see me soon, I realized that our journey was just beginning. As I looked up at him,

I was glad things didn't work on my timeline because if I was right about him, and he was the man I thought he was, there was nothing that would keep us apart. Whatever it was, I knew things would work themselves out.

No, my life was not perfect, and I still had my insecurities, but I was grateful for the chance to do what I loved and help mentor others along the way. I was also grateful for my health and my family and friends who loved me. I'd learned a lot of hard lessons throughout the years, but I realized I was stronger because of everything I'd been through; I knew it was necessary for a time such as this. I was now experiencing more joy than I ever dreamed of. My time was now, and that made this moment truly worth the wait.

Thank you for reading Worth the Weight: A Love Like No Other. I truly hope that you enjoyed Anisa's journey, and that you feel inspired after reading her story. Look out for several of her friends and family's journey in the near future. If you've enjoyed the book, please don't forget to leave a review everywhere books are sold!

www.bn.com
www.amazon.com
www.goodreads.com

ACKNOWLEDGEMENTS

I began writing this book in May 2020, and I'm not afraid to say that it went in a different direction after the killing of George Floyd on May 25th. Most of the businesses mentioned are Black-owned because I figured that rather than making up names, I should give love to more Black-owned establishments; we often get looked over. Each entity mentioned—with the exception of Iya's Gems—is a real establishment, so make sure to support them if you're in Miami or the DMV area, or support them online.

So, here it goes: To my Black-owned establishments in every form, I see you and I'm happy to join you in showing what we can do! In case you don't hear it enough, thank you! Thank you! Thank you! You are my inspiration. There are so many who don't get their just due, but I'm glad to do my small part in showcasing a few and reminding the world that we are here to stay, no matter what opposition we face.

To my beautiful queens, if anyone has made you feel less than or made you question your value or self-worth, whether it be a family member or significant other who tried to steal your shine, know that God didn't put you on this earth to be anything less than the amazing human being that you are. Now get up and illuminate the way for someone else, because you were meant for greatness.

To my friends, family, and mentors for their encouragement—you put up with me while I was writing like crazy, and I appreciate you! Thanks for your patience and letting me use you as test dummies time and time again. You all know who you are and what you did for me. Love you!

Thank God for the gift of writing and for those who helped me rediscover my gift. Sorry that I took so long to use it, but I'm putting in overtime now.

Last but certainly not least: Thank you, Lord, for keeping me even when I didn't want to be kept.

QUESTIONS AND TOPICS FOR DISCUSSION

1. Do you feel the pressure of societal norms in regards to your career, marriage, etc., or do you feel that things will happen when they are supposed to?
2. How do you feel about the way Anisa handled the situation when she found out about Terrence's other relationship? Do you agree with her contacting Asha when she found out that Terrence was still married? Do you agree with how both ladies handled the situation? What would you have done differently?
3. In the novel, Anisa and Asha seem to form a bond. Do you think that situation is realistic considering the way they were introduced to each other?
4. Anisa's family and friends were very involved with her love life with Terrence. Do you feel that they were too involved? How would/do you deal with close friends and family when you know a relationship isn't right for them?
5. Have you ever been in a relationship that most of your friends and family disapproved of? What ended up being the outcome of that situation?

6. Do you think Zahair was moving too quickly even though they dated in college? Would you have chosen to relocate for love in that instance, especially after a recent breakup?
7. Do you feel that Zahair was too overbearing and gave up on their relationship too quickly? Why do you think she resisted being with him? Have you ever felt unworthy of being with someone?
8. Who was your favorite character in the story, and why? Which character's journey would you like to see next?
9. Do you thoroughly vet a person that you get involved with (background checks, Google searches, etc.)? What's the most you've ever done to find out about a man/woman?
10. Do you feel childhood trauma still drives most of the decisions you make in your life? Do you recognize habits you have formed from childhood that you need to break in order to become better? If so, what are you doing to make those changes?
11. Do you think Anisa and Zahair will end up together? If so, who do you think should make the move?
12. Do you feel as though you're living out your purpose and following your passion(s)? If not, do you know what your passion is, and if so, what have you done to fulfill it?

Visit Keisha WriteNow Allen online:

Tag me with a picture of you and the book (with good lighting please), so I can post you to my page and give a shout out!

Facebook *@Keisha WriteNow Allen*
Instagram *@keisha_writenow_allen*
Twitter *@KeishaWriteNow*

Visit my website: *www.keishawritenowallen.com*

Here you can:

- Find out about contests and prizes
- Find out more about my writing journey
- Learn about upcoming books
- And much more